t4

MDCC
10

BLIND GEESE

By the same Author:

WINIFRED DUKE

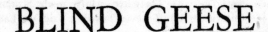

BLIND GEESE

*" It is a blind goose that goes
to the fox's sermon "*

JARROLDS *Publishers* (LONDON) *Ltd.*

Founded in 1770

47 Princes Gate, S.W.7

LONDON * NEW YORK * MELBOURNE * SYDNEY

"Deluded prince! how is thy greatness crost,
And all the gaudy dream of empire lost,
That proudly set thee on a fancy'd throne,
And made imaginary realms thy own!"

JOSEPH ADDISON: *The Campaign.*

"Then came the year 'Forty-five, which made Scotland to be talked of everywhere; but I never heard it said we had anyway gained by the 'Forty-five."

R. L. S.: *Catriona.*

"Fierce midnights and famishing morrows."

A. C. SWINBURNE.

"Much the same judgment may be made of the Prince's whole expedition by any person that considers the various difficulties he had to struggle with. If he did less at Culloden than was expected from him, 'twas only because he had formerly done more than could be expected."

MAXWELL OF KIRKCONNELL.

"The rebels published accounts of the battles of Preston and Falkirk, in which they were victorious; but no account of the battle of Culloden has been published by the vanquished."

JOHN HOME.

"Cæsar armed, with the eyes of a falcon."

DANTE: *Inferno*, iv. 121-123.

MADE AND PRINTED IN GREAT BRITAIN AT
THE FLEET STREET PRESS
EAST HARDING STREET, E.C.4
1946

CHAPTER I

IT WAS THE EVENING OF THE FIFTEENTH OF APRIL, 1746.
The night was dooms-dark and winter cold. Half of the month had gone by, yet the wind sat persistently in the east, buds were still sealed secretively, and the air felt harsh, sunless. There had been long rain, which left the ground soaked and spongy. Now and again a sleepy bird twittered; otherwise the silence hung as motionless, as unrevealing as the silence after death. Death, indeed, lurked much in the minds of all this night, though another beside him trod at the heels of a body of tired, dispirited men. His name was Hunger, and he gnawed into lean bodies until nothing save the satisfying of him seemed to matter.

Lieutenant Ranald Cameron was with others of his clan. Under their chief Lochiel they followed the Atholl Brigade, led by Lord George Murray, who had undertaken to head this night-march for the purpose of attacking the Duke of Cumberland's forces, encamped at Nairn, some twelve miles away. The young Highlander shrugged his shoulders. It was a mad scheme, but what else could they do? The Prince's army was depleted, his officers at variance with one another, his men, for the last month paid only in meal, discontented and slyly deserting on every opportunity, whilst no succours worth mentioning had come from France. The whole rising was a madness, a chimera, a long-drawn-out nightmare, yet it was fantastic to picture it as ending in disaster and defeat. Charles Edward's men had beaten Cope at Gladsmuir and routed Hawley at Falkirk, not to speak of that gallant dash into the heart of England. Was this fat Hanoverian, with his picked troops, his fine artillery, his strategy, his preparations, to win when pitted against the ill-equipped, semi-starved motley army of the Prince? And defeat meant—— He shivered, despite his plaid and his strong, young body, habituated to the austerities of this harsh northern climate. Cold held no terrors for his hardy frame, but the thought of possible mutilation by a Whig broadsword or bayonet, capture, trial, and public execution chilled his warm blood.

Only nine months earlier Scotland had been at ease, troubled by rumours, no doubt, and watching with indifferent gaze the progress of events on the Continent where war raged, but her own soil lay undisturbed. For so long now, old men told one another, there had been talk of a rising in favour of the exiled house of Stuart, but it was no more than talk. James III and VIII was a pious, priest-ridden dreamer. After his futile throw in 1715 he had had the wisdom, save for that botched business four years later, to make no attempt to regain the throne of Great Britain. Ay, but he had sons, younger men muttered. Tales stole to Scotland of the elder Prince's strength and daring. Only the previous year he had been in France, summoned by the French king, and nothing save the weather had wrecked his hopes of sailing with the vast fleet destined to attack England. After that a cloud of obscurity, dense, impenetrable, covered his movements. He was said to be lurking at Gravelines, hiding in Paris, or even, some declared, returned ignominiously to Rome. Murray of Broughton, that sly, smooth-spoken Lowlander, who until a few weeks ago had served the Prince as secretary throughout his campaign, went to and fro between the Scottish and the French capitals, conveying letters, carrying promises, bearing word of a Prince who only waited for his country to summon him. "Though I bring but a single footman with me, I shall visit Scotland next summer!" he told Murray. Well, he had not brought much more, the young Cameron reflected sourly.

The ground underfoot was little better than a bog. His feet squelched in and out of black liquid mud. How slowly the two long columns marched!

He was the eldest son. His family were Jacobite rather because they followed their Chief in politics than from any hereditary or personal inclination towards the Stuarts. From childhood young Ranald had learned to drink to the King over the water, to think of George II as the Elector of Hanover, and to pity Lochiel whose father had paid by lifelong exile from Scotland for his share in that muddled and stupid affair styled the '15, but a Stuart restoration meant little to him. He and his father nursed the small estate which called the former laird into something resembling prosperity. The change of season—long, cold weeks of spring—springs unlike this one, he recalled sullenly—summers always with a touch of sharpness in the wine-strong air, calm, mellow autumns, when bracken yellowed on the high hillsides, and winters of interminable length—through these, year after year, he had watched the land ripen and change, seen the fields heavy for harvest, the cattle being fattened for market, known all the stir and life and growth—plant and animal—about a Highland holding. He was twenty-five and contented, thinking himself in love, when the summons came——

It was a very still August day. The heat-mist hid the mountain-tops, and the humming of insects made a monotonous orchestra in the close air. He had been down in a field by the loch when a sound of shouting drew his attention to a man of the clan running towards him. From the fellow's confused Gaelic, Ranald made out that he was wanted. His father had received news—great news.

"But what is it, Shemus?"

"They are saying that the Prince has landed!"

"Landed? Which Prince?"

"Prince Tearlach, King Jamie's son."

Ranald stood motionless. To the end of his life (possibly no long one now, he realized, with grim conviction) he should remember that moment. Overhead a buzzard sailed, a dim speck in the vast area of cloudless blue. A cow was lowing, and a branch of rowans, already scarlet, hung over the dyke. Growing corn was the height of a man's waist. The whole immediate landscape seemed strident with colour, fading into the long stretches of purple where heather thatched the moorland. The wind was warm, caressing. Gaunt pines fringed the loch in which he had fished and bathed since boyhood——

"And—— Where, Shemus?" he stammered.

"I do not know."

He stumbled towards the house, his brain busy with pictures of a vast invading army, at its head the fairy-tale Prince, Tearlach, as the Gael styled him. Was he to leave all this to fight for Charles? The place tugged at his heart-strings. His father was not old, as years went, but he had halted since a fall from an unmanageable horse five years earlier. Must he, the first-born, go in his stead? His thoughts went to his clan-chief. Which way would Lochiel decide? At his call all able-bodied men bearing the name and badge of Cameron must follow, were bound to follow. If not—— It was high summer, yet Ranald shivered, as he caught himself shivering now, when he recalled tales whispered about the horrors of that earlier rising, burned roof-tree, homeless peasantry, dispossessed crofters, all suffering for a Cause they neither understood nor sympathized with.

The house was white-harled, its walls and angles clear against the dark tapestry of a small fir-wood on the rising ground behind. Ranald saw his father waiting, certain of the clan gathered about the door, a few women, including his mother, whispering and weeping, all listening to the newcomer. He was a tall Highlander, wearing the Cameron tartan.

Ranald plunged into the group.

"Speak!" he cried. "The Prince has landed?"

"Ay," answered the Cameron.

Ranald nodded to him to continue.

Lochiel, the messenger explained, had received a letter, summoning him to Borradale in Arisaig. The Prince had arrived there.

"With what support?"

The Highlander's fine teeth showed in a grim laugh. "Neither money, arms, nor men."

"Madness!" muttered Ranald.

"Ay. So Lochiel thought."

"But he was pledged to go out," struck in the elder Cameron.

"Only if the Prince brought aid. He has none."

The tale went on. Lochiel started for Borradale, but on the way called at Fassefern, the house of his brother. The latter, a shrewd business man, wondered at this unexpected visit. What was the matter bringing Donald there at so early an hour? Lochiel admitted that the Prince had landed and sent for him. What support had he? Fassefern demanded. Lochiel answered reluctantly that he believed Charles had brought with him no troops, money, or arms. He added that he himself was resolved not to be concerned in the affair and to persuade Charles to abandon the enterprise. Fassefern approved this firmness. Strongly he recommended his brother to go no farther, but to come into the house and write the Prince a letter conveying his decision.

"And Lochiel agreed?"

"No. He replied that at least he ought to wait upon the Prince and give his Royal Highness his reasons for declining to join him, which admitted of no reply."

"What said Fassefern?"

"Fassefern laughed and told Lochiel that he knew him better than Lochiel knew himself. 'If this Prince once sets his eyes upon you, he will make you do whatever he pleases,' were his words."

"Yet Lochiel went to Borradale?"

"Yes."

Ranald plodded on through the black mud. Ahead, he saw Lochiel, walking steadily. What thoughts were in his mind? Did he regret his past weakness in yielding to Charles's importunities, his charm, his claims? Afterwards Ranald learned of that first encounter between the Cameron chief and Tearlach and could, from his own subsequent experience of the Prince, realize how Charles's grace and subtle argument had won over even Lochiel's prudence and common sense. He could picture the Prince, flushed, youthful, pacing to and fro, his long hands gesticulating vehemently, his fair head thrown back proudly, words pouring from his lips. He spoke violently, bitterly of the treatment meted out to him by the French ministers. Their promises were vain things. Wearied of inaction and skulking, he had taken matters into his own grasp and come over, inflamed by the promises of his father's brave and faithful subjects to assist him. Lochiel admitted that the chiefs had engaged to support a rising, but as the Prince had landed without aid of any kind they were absolved from their pledge. Firmly he told the Prince that his Royal Highness had not the least prospect of success. The only course was for him to return to France and await a more favourable opportunity.

The Prince had refused stubbornly to accept Lochiel's advice. A more favourable opportunity than the present one would never come, he averred hotly. Almost all the British troops were abroad, kept at bay by Marshal Saxe. In Scotland the few newly raised regiments, unaccustomed to war, would never be able to stand before the Highlanders. Once they began the campaign his father's friends at home would declare themselves, and friends abroad contribute their assistance. He only waited for the Highlands to rise.

Lochiel had continued to resist. Would not the Prince at least consent to remain concealed at Borradale until Lochiel and others could meet to discuss the position and decide what was best to be done? Charles answered that he was determined to hazard all. "In a few days," he had cried, "with the few friends that I have, I will erect the royal standard, and proclaim to the people of Britain that Charles Stuart is come over to claim the crown of his ancestors, to win it, or to perish in the attempt. Lochiel, who, as my father has often told me, was our firmest friend, may stay at home, and learn from the newspapers the fate of his Prince."

"And Lochiel? What said he to this?"

The Highlander's dark eyes glowed. He answered: "'No. I'll share the fate of my Prince; and so shall every man over whom nature or fortune hath given me any power'."

The older Cameron glanced at his son. "We shall both go, Ranald."

In this chill April night it was difficult to recall the burning heat of that August day when the standard had been unfurled at Glenfinnan. The young man strove to picture the scene now: the narrow vale, with the river running between high mountains, the blue of the sky mirrored in the deep loch at either end, the hot air fanning the waiting faces, the tall, regal young figure which emerged from a rude hovel in which the Prince had been waiting restlessly for the past two hours. Ah! he was bonnie then, slight and fair-haired, bronzed already by the sun, but now—— Ranald glanced round uneasily. The long column was divided into two portions and the Prince rode between these. He was thin and changed, the glow and certainty which had haloed him earlier dimmed by the mists of suspicion and semi-failure. What was in his mind? Did he regret that he had withstood Lochiel's entreaties, flouted his advice, and gone forward, despite opposition, refusals, warning whispers of the madness of the enterprise? None could tell. He confided in few, and these were not the Scots. Ranald Cameron's supple mouth curled derisively as he thought of those men whom the Prince chose to make his intimates. Sir Thomas Sheridan, his former tutor; Colonel O'Sullivan, his quartermaster-general, Irish and plausible, on whose broad shoulders must rest the greater share of responsibility for the muddle and mismanagement of the commissariat; Murray of Broughton, negligible now through his ill-health; Hay of Restalrig, who had taken Murray's place and insinuated himself into Charles's good graces to Murray's helpless wrath—these were his friends, whereas others—— Ranald bit his lip savagely. What had the Irish to lose? A French commission protected many of them, whilst the Scots—— From Lord George Murray downward each risked his all: estate, fortune, security, life itself. The Prince might say that equally with these others he had everything at stake, as well as a great price upon his head, but the night's hazard menaced each man more than it did their young leader. Ranald hunched his shoulders. How had it fallen to this? Once the initial difficulties after the landing were overcome the Prince had succeeded—succeeded beyond the most sanguine hopes. He had struck southward, taken Edinburgh, defeated Cope, reigned in brief triumph for six weeks at Holyrood, invaded England, investing Carlisle, Manchester, a score of smaller towns, and entered Derby. Derby! A memory wrenched at the young man's heart of the wet, unwelcoming town, the sullen inhabitants, the news that it had been decided to face about and return to Scotland, the Prince's rage and despair, the Highlanders' disappointed wrath. The retreat was a blurred mosaic of deplorable roads ankle-deep in mud, slush, or snow, the sense of flight with foes at their heels, growing dissensions and disagreements amongst the leaders. The crazy folly of leaving a force to garrison Carlisle! Those bitter weeks of winter, retreating, ever retreating, the prevailing failure and chagrin, lightened only by the fleeting victory at Falkirk, the last small successes such as the fall of Inverness and the sub-duing of Fort Augustus, and the final dragging weeks until Cumberland struck. Would this night's venture end all? What chance was there of striking down the Hanoverian camp?

He thought prosaically instead of his ever-present hunger. There was meal in abundance at Inverness, but at Culloden House a biscuit apiece had been the ration that day for officers and men alike. The Prince had fared little better. It was a dark, louring morning, with rain-laden mist hiding the mountain peaks and chilling tired bodies. The army, drawn up in battle array, looked, Ranald reflected cynically, more like a horde of starving and desperate outlaws than a force which had conquered half Scotland. Lord George Murray disliked the place chosen as a battle-ground. It was not proper for Highlanders, he argued. He proposed crossing the river and making a stand on the boggy, hilly country beyond, where the enemy's horse and cannon would be rendered useless. Charles and his party had disagreed. After scouts who had gone to Nairn returned with a report that all was quiet there it had been decided to dismiss the men and let them go in search of food. This had depleted the ranks so severely that when the time came to muster for the night-march at least two thousand were missing. For a space the fate of the enterprise hung in the balance. Only the Prince's feverish insistence had won the day. The long columns trudged away through a wood beside a defile, silent, dulled by hunger and despair to an apathetic acquiescence in whatever might befall. No blink of star or hint of moon broke the blackness. It was very cold.

Half stupefied, Ranald Cameron became aware that the foremost column was sagging to a halt. Word ran along that the gap between the lines was too great. The first must march slower. As in a dream he heard the voices of Lord George and others raised in argument. How long had the army been tramping through mud? It seemed an incalculable space of time, yet was probably not above an hour. More than any-thing else he longed for rest. He glanced at the patient men, realized that he might have to stand indefinitely, and lurching out of the line, subsided on a part of the ground less boggy than the track. He did not intend to sleep. He must not. A few minutes' repose, a little space in which to pull himself together —who would grudge him these?

CHAPTER II

MR. JOHN HAY OF RESTALRIG WAS IN THE VAN WITH SUNDRY others. At times this grim march seemed like some fragment—a very large one—from a nightmare out of which it became impossible to awake. Was it sober truth that he, a respectable Writer to the Signet, brother to Thomas Hay of Huntington, that rising Edinburgh advocate, bound to ascend the judicial bench one day, could be riding through squelching mud, a haar-laden wind in his unprotected face, one of a desperate band of men making their last throw? The position was unsuitable, grotesque. His profession was the Law; his speciality figures. It was twenty years since his admission to that select legal body the Edinburgh Writers to the Signet, and his world through the ensuing two decades had been bounded by the duties and interests involved in tending his estate of Restalrig, outside the Scottish capital, the Parliament House, the coffee-houses and taverns of Edinburgh where men of Law forgathered, and his position as Substitute-Keeper of the Signet, fiscal, and treasurer. How did he come to be in this disagreeable and disadvantageous situation? Sourly he blamed the Prince's previous secretary whom he had succeeded a few weeks earlier. Murray of Broughton was a violent Jacobite and his sister had married Mr. Hay's brother, the aspirant to a judge's scarlet-crossed white satin. Through Mr. Murray, Mr. Hay knew perfectly well what had been going on for over a year before the Prince's landing. He could not plead ignorance, or lament that he had been over-persuaded, against his better judgment, to join the Stuart party. Neither was he pressed into Charles's service. No—Mr. Hay ground his teeth —he happened to be here entirely owing to his own fault. If he had remained in his comfortable semi-obscurity, content with Court of Session business, the affairs discussed in Parliament Hall, the secrets confided and the views exchanged over a morning dram with other advocates in Johnnie Dowie's tavern, probably he would have died in his bed at a ripe old age, instead of being dispatched, a comparatively young man, by Hanoverian bayonet or judicial execution as a traitor.

This night-attack on Cumberland's camp was madness. Mr. Hay's opinion had not been even solicited beforehand; otherwise he would certainly have voted strongly against the scheme. The Prince and Lord George were for once in agreement when each spoke of it as a desirable possibility, but Mr. Hay distrusted the motives of both. His Royal Highness, impulsive, enthusiastic, saw in it a decisive victory. My Lord George, grimly disillusioned, realized that it offered an alternative to fighting on that bare, sodden plateau near the river. Had he something else in his mind? Mr. Hay wondered. As man and soldier, Lord George impelled his unwilling admiration, but the Prince's dislike and distrust of his able Lieutenant-General had seeped into Mr. Hay's mentality until he came to look upon Lord George through Charles's eyes. In addition he was disagreeably aware that Lord George regarded Colonel John Hay as a mighty poor substitute for Murray of Broughton, however much he and Murray had hated one another.

His thoughts went back over the past months as his horse stumbled and thrust its way through the boggy surface of the road.

From the start—unconsciously his lean chest expanded proudly—he had been an important figure in the Prince's councils. At Perth, where he first joined the Royal Adventurer, others might be allotted posts of greater administrative responsibility, but Prince Charles had early recognized Mr. Hay's worth, integrity, and ability, and utilized the same. He knew what was planned when the Jacobite army left the Fair City. Glasgow was a rich morsel to men owning poverty-stricken Highland estates. So far the second city in Scotland, out of its twenty thousand inhabitants, had not contributed anything in men or money to advance the Prince's Cause. Glasgow was Whig, rebellious, and, incidentally, very frightened. As the rebels drew nearer her Lord Provost was sending abject appeals for help to Edinburgh, but the Lord Justice-Clerk and General Guest, in command of the garrison at Edinburgh Castle, were too occupied by their own troubles—immediate and prospective—to heed the wails from the west. Never had the Law lords or the civic authorities of the capital imagined that a rising would come to this. Wild rumours had circulated, following the delayed information of the landing. One morning it was confidently affirmed that Charles had arrived in one of the Western Isles with ten thousand men. The following day it had been given out with equal conviction that he was in the Highlands without any troops, but that the Highlanders to a man had risen to support him. Three thousand French were landed at the Goose Dub, a puddle near the meadow of Edinburgh. Sir John Cope had marched to meet the invaders, but there had been no battle. Now he was at Inverness, and the Jacobites, gathering strength, had moved southward. What would be their next objective? Glasgow shook in its shoes. Edinburgh awaited in terror huge hordes of imperfectly armed savages. Mr. Hay smiled. Was it not his adroitness, his sagacity, his well-timed advice which had persuaded the Prince to send a demand to Glasgow, but to advance in person upon Edinburgh? At Lecky House he himself drafted the letter for the Glasgow magistrates and their Provost. He did it well, too, as befitted one learned in the Law.

Lecky was reached on a mellow September afternoon. The Highland scenery might be glorious and majestic, but Mr. Hay, laird of Restalrig, thought very decidedly that the Lowlands had great beauty of their own. A little mist dimmed the sharpness of the air and the brightness of the slowly turning foliage. The brambles in the hedgerows were purple-black against the dust-white of the ripe oats and the pale yellow of the barley stooks. The rowans were a strident red and the cornfields a gold tapestry. The Prince, who had waded across the Forth at the Fords of Frew, arrived on horseback, very gallant and gracious. The laird of Lecky should have been on the steps to welcome his Royal Highness, but the laird of Lecky, it transpired, was unavoidably absent. A hint as to his intention of entertaining the Young Chevalier had unfortunately crept abroad, and a party of soldiers had arrived the previous night and carried the luckless George Moir to Stirling Castle. Happily the dinner had been ordered in good time and the wines were an admirable choice; otherwise the episode would have had an even more unpleasant complexion. Mr. Hay sighed.

Mellowed by food and drink, the Prince's followers held an informal council after the meal. Charles had been alternatively pensive and excited. Furtively the man of Law studied him as he chattered volubly or sat sunk in an abstracted silence. Was he realizing more and more fully the perils and hazards of his enterprise? Did it come home to him that he had left behind the friendly shelter of the Highlands, together with their mountains and glens, and was in the Lowlands, indifferent, if not actively hostile to his Cause and claims? Mr. Hay had dared to interrupt his Royal Highness's brooding thoughts. With all due submission to the advice of wiser heads —he recalled shooting a glance of barely veiled dislike at Lord George Murray—he ventured to propose——

The Prince had raised his chin and sat up. "Eh? You would say, *mon cher*——?"

"That if your Royal Highness designs to march upon Glasgow——"

"Had we concerted to do so, gentlemen?"

The rest murmured cautious nothings. No definite plan had been agreed upon. The choice lay between advancing towards Edinburgh and summoning the city to surrender, or investing Glasgow, with its fat purses. It was for the Prince Regent to make the decision.

"What is Mr. Hay's advice?" Charles asked.

Mr. Hay, diffident and abashed, proffered his opinion. If Edinburgh became the Jacobites' objective, then Glasgow should not congratulate itself on escaping. A sum of money— a large one—ought to be extracted from the citizens. Murmurs of approbation followed Charles's eager assent. A letter must be drafted, addressed to the Provost and magistrates.

Again Mr. Hay sat in modest silence whilst the terms of the document were discussed. How much to demand? Five thousand? Ten? Fifteen? The latter sum met with the royal and general consent. In addition, all the city's arms were to be delivered up, and in case of disobedience the greatest severities were threatened. At the Prince's request Mr. Hay drew up the letter, and after it had been read and approved by all present Charles appended his large, sprawling signature.

Once more Mr. Hay smiled, despite the increasing cold of his feet, his empty stomach, and the undoubted danger and unpleasantness ahead. Eh, but he had shaken the complacency of those fat Glasgow burgesses! Armed with the letter, and the Prince's signed commission to deliver it, Mr. Hay set forth next morning, in company with Captain Roy MacDonald, a kinsman of Kinlochmoidart's, and rode to Glasgow.

The city was quaking and appalled. Mr. Hay gathered the depth of the prevailing fears as he delivered Charles's missive to the magistrates. The latter summoned their principal inhabitants to discuss the horrifying demand. Glasgow was thoroughly scared, Mr. Hay realized, with the rebels, at least four thousand strong, barely twelve miles away, and the wild Highlanders only too ready for plunder and destruction.

The authorities temporized, and finally sent a deputation to beg the rebels for leniency. By the time it reached Kilsyth the Prince and his followers were heading for Edinburgh. Mr. Hay glanced back wistfully to the brief splendours of that time. The capital fell by strategy, without the drawing of a broadsword or the firing of a shot. In a blaze of triumph, Charles entered the dark, low-lying palace of his ancestors. The Law lords had fled. On the whole the populace was enthusiastic and admiring, the Whig element keeping discreetly to the background. A few days later the Highland army met and defeated Sir John Cope's returned forces at Gladsmuir, and Charles was master of the city. Guards were placed at Leith and Newhaven, patrolling the shore to prevent parties from landing from the men-of-war in the Forth. Other guards stood at Inch to watch the south road, at Jock's Lodge to observe the road from Berwick, at the Weigh-house at the head of the Lawnmarket to keep the castle under surveillance, and likewise at the West Kirk and Livingston's Yards. Edinburgh was forced to contribute tents, military stores, and arms. Holyrood was a hive of busyness. The magistrates of the boroughs, the Collector of Taxes, the Controller of Customs were all summoned there "upon pain of rebellion and high treason," and most of them compelled to obey. Unfortunately money was becoming a paramount need, and Mr. Hay had to be dispatched to Glasgow a second time.

The recollection made him grin, despite his present circumstances. Again he had interviewed the civic authorities and after a long and acrimonious discussion agreed to modify the original demand of fifteen thousand pounds to five thousand, five hundred sterling. But this was not all. After the retreat from Derby—Mr. Hay scowled—the Prince had marched to Glasgow and spent eight days there. His Royal Highness was, as a rule, inclined to be too lenient, Mr. Hay decided, but on this occasion he had made Glasgow pay for its disloyalty and stubborn adherence to the House of Hanover. Once again Mr. Hay had had the pleasure of arriving in advance and stating the extent of the Prince Regent's threats. How greatly he had enjoyed walking into the clerk's chamber where the magistrates and some of the principal citizens were assembled, quaking, all in a bonnie twitter, and making them listen to a long harangue. Mr. Hay lectured Glasgow on its late rebellion and appearance in arms, its unnatural conduct in marching a battalion to Stirling, and concluded by saying that in order to strike a terror into other places his Royal

Highness was resolved to make Glasgow an example of his just severity. The citizens were left in acute suspense until Charles, with the clans, had actually arrived, and then Mr. Hay summoned the magistrates and chief inhabitants to notify his Royal Highness's pleasure. Glasgow was to be fined in six thousand cloth short coats, twelve thousand linen shirts, six thousand pairs of shoes, six thousand bonnets, and as many tartan hose, besides a sum of money. In vain did the authorities remonstrate against these demands which they impudently characterized as exorbitant, and represented that as most of these goods were not in the town they were unable to furnish or pay. Mr. Hay merely answered that the citizens were rebels and must perform all this on pain of military execution. For fear of being plundered the cravens ultimately agreed to do all in their power, but Mr. Hay greatly resented certain of the important counsellors going behind his back to Lord George Murray, Lochiel, and several others, who had the assurance to say that they condemned the measure, but Mr. Hay had fixed the Prince in his resolution of adhering to the demand. Ah, ha! his influence over Charles was already becoming realized and resented.

Once again his thoughts reverted from Glasgow to Edinburgh and the Prince's transient triumphs there. More and more support flooded in. The Prince held state at Holyrood, presiding over a daily council of his officers and chiefs, reviewing his troops, receiving the fair ladies who flocked to his court. It was a mad time of glamour and surface success, but underneath ran dark currents——

Mr. Hay held no great opinion of his connection by marriage and fellow-secretary, Mr. Murray of Broughton. In the first place, if it had not been for Mr. Murray's secret encouragement, despite all his denials of the same, the Prince might never have come to Scotland. Occasionally, when he was tired, overworked, or vapourish, Mr. Hay regretted acutely that his Royal Highness had. Mr. Murray was decidedly inclined to keep the Prince to himself, to be deep in the royal confidence, to exclude others whom he did not trust. This last included Lord George Murray, against whom Mr. Murray had poisoned the Prince's mind as early as Perth. In any case, reflected Mr. Hay, the Prince and Lord George would never have pulled together amiably. Lord George was hot-tempered, blunt, tactless, and dictatorial. He had a stiff manner, a plain tongue, a deeply-rooted distrust of the Irish element in Charles's entourage, and the Prince's half-foreign excitability,

B

his rashness in embarking on the most hazardous enterprises without counting the cost perpetually vexed and exasperated Lord George. If the two seemed on a better footing, then, mused Mr. Hay, Mr. Murray was always ready to drop a hint to the Prince that Lord George's loyalty was suspect, or to repeat to Lord George some uncomplimentary criticism made about him by Sir Thomas Sheridan or Colonel O'Sullivan in the Prince's hearing.

Those Irish! Mr. Hay did not like any of them. He had rejoiced secretly when the Reverend George Kelly, a bad influence upon his Royal Highness since the days of their association in Paris, had been sent back to France with dispatches.

The daily council usually meant friction. To his secret chagrin, Mr. Hay was not a member of it, but he could generally learn afterwards from someone who was what had passed. Mr. Murray was clever, eh! very clever. Never openly siding with either, he invariably managed to set the Prince and Lord George at variance with one another. He said very little. Later it would be impossible to recollect the precise word or hint or look or brief comment which fired the two combustible elements. Mr. Hay frowned. He knew that he owed his own position with the Prince largely to Mr. Murray's good offices, but Mr. Murray had not presented the advocate to his Royal Highness from wholly disinterested motives. *Non, non, non!* as the Prince would have exclaimed. There were others whom Mr. Murray feared, single-hearted, influential, important, and what danger was there from Mr. Hay of Restalrig? Mr. Murray was no fool. He saw that the Prince required to be tactfully handled, managed, governed, and swayed, and had performed these offices himself to perfection until illness laid him aside. This was Mr. Hay's opportunity and one which he was not slow to seize.

A wind whined through the trees. Irritably he moved his stone-cold feet in the stirrups. How long had this dreary march lasted? It seemed hours, days, weeks, months, years——

Surely the column ahead of him, nothing but a solid mass in the enveloping darkness, had come to a halt? He could distinguish voices, but no words. Those sounded like Lord George Murray's deep tones, against Lochiel's softer ones, and the broad Scottish accents of the Duke of Perth. What was toward? Mr. Hay thrust his horse forward. He was an important figure, deep in the Prince's confidence. No step ought to be taken without consulting him, soliciting his opinion, deferring to his advice. If a serious decision were under discussion he should be there to state his views. Why had not Lord George Murray dispatched a message summoning him, requesting his presence?

The little group stood in the blackness beyond the first column. Lord John Drummond, the Duke of Perth's brother, was speaking loudly, angrily. "Why will you go on? There is a gap in the line half a mile long. The men won't come up."

"Then what do you advise?" Lord George gave a curt order to halt.

Mr. Hay, in growing concern, watched O'Sullivan, Mr. Hepburn of Keith, and other volunteers who had marched all night in the first column, join the rest and begin to air their opinions. Repeating watches were drawn out and consulted. Two o'clock! Increasing lightness in the sky, a grey glimmer behind the trees confirmed that a great many hours had elapsed since the columns left Culloden House at eight o'clock the previous night. Nairn was still more than three miles off. From the time they had taken to reach their present objective it was disagreeably evident that it would be broad daylight before Nairn could be approached. Lord George Murray said briefly:

"This is a free parliament, gentlemen. I desire everybody to give his opinion, for we are all equally concerned."

A babel of voices and argument broke out.

"I advise a retreat."

"Ay, as daylight is so near, and we cannot expect to surprise the enemy."

"True. That is the only wise course."

"Sir, to retreat will not advantage us. We shall only have to fight the Duke a few hours hence."

"Let us march on to Nairn. I'll wager my men are keen when once informed of what is toward."

"Madness!" shouted Lord George.

"Nay, why, my lord? I agree with Dr. Cameron."

"Pray, Lord George, lose no time, but order the men to march on to Nairn as fast as they can."

The last speaker was Mr. Hepburn of Keith. Mr. Hay did not like him and resented his thrusting himself forward so positively. Because he had walked before the Prince Regent, carrying his drawn sword, when Charles entered Holyrood for the first time did not entitle him to oppose his opinion to Lord George Murray's, to instruct Lord George what course to follow, although Lord George had no right to take it upon himself to order a retreat. What folly, after they had come thus far! Mr. Hay felt exceedingly angry. He must intervene ere it became too late.

A dull, muffled sound broke the damp stillness. Members of the little group started and looked at one another. Mr. Hepburn of Keith ceased abruptly to speak.

"A drum!"

"Don't you hear? The enemy are alarmed. We can't surprise them." Lord George's tones matched his haggard face.

"I never expected to find them asleep." Mr. Hepburn of Keith squared his shoulders. "But it is much better to march on and attack them than to retreat, for they will most certainly follow and oblige us to fight when we shall be in a much worse condition for battle than we are now."

Lord George retorted angrily. There were approving murmurs from those who favoured his plan of retiring to Culloden. Others supported Mr. Hepburn, still pressing his point of view. Mr. Hay joined the group, demanding to be informed of what was afoot.

Lord George answered curtly.

"We are retreating, sir. The resolution is taken to return to Culloden House."

"But the attack, my lord? The Prince?"

"His Royal Highness will be informed of the decision, sir."

"He will never consent."

"Is he in any situation to object to my dispositions, Mr. Hay?"

" 'Tis contrary to what was agreed upon."

Mr. Hay was very wroth with the reception accorded to his views. Lord George Murray and the rest did not seem to have the faintest idea of what was due to the Prince's secretary. He argued angrily that there would be time to make the attack, that everything had been concerted for it, and implied plainly that Lord George Murray had no right to take upon himself to alter the pre-arranged plan. None heeded. Even to his own ears his voice and protests sounded thin, ineffective, devitalized, feeble. Well, he had one weapon left. The Prince must deal with this unprecedented, unlooked-for situation, and Mr. Hay was the proper person to inform him of what was brewing behind his back.

Charles was in the centre of the line of march. Turning his horse ostentatiously upon the group surrounding Lord George Murray, Mr. Hay made the best of his way to the

Prince's side. The sky was slowly fading from dense black to a uniform grey against which an occasional object stood out: a man's face, white and strained, a tall, stripped tree, a tracery of branches still leafless and bleak, the uneven line of a broken wall. As he approached he saw the horse on which the Prince was mounted stamping restlessly, and heard Charles's quick, high voice. "What is this delay? We should press on. It must be near sunrise."

"Sir?" Mr. Hay stole nearer, thrusting aside those who would have barred his progress to the Prince.

"Eh? Who is it? Why, Mr. Hay!"

"Sir, unless your Royal Highness comes to the front and orders Lord George Murray to go on, nothing will be done."

"I do not understand. *Comment?*"

"Lord George has ordered the men to retreat, sir."

"*Mon Dieu!* To retreat?"

Charles stared at Mr. Hay. Long years of a close association were still to lie before them, but the secretary never forgot the Prince as he saw him at that moment. The long, high-bred face, pallid and worn so that the cheek-bones thrust outwards sharply, the startled amazement and incredulity in the darkly circled eyes, the puzzled lift of proud, arched brows, the sudden clenching of the hand on the bridle. Then the Prince thrust in the spurs and, regardless of whom he rode down in his path, galloped recklessly forward through the wan dawn.

CHAPTER III

CHARLES WAS CONSCIOUS OF LITTLE EXCEPT A BLIND ANGER, shaking his whole body like physical sickness. Was it credible, possible that this scheme of his, conceived so cunningly and carefully, planned so secretively, approved of by Lord George, and ripe for its fulfilment, was about to be abandoned altogether? He groaned aloud. "I am betrayed. What need to give orders when my orders are disobeyed?" Only the silence of the wood answered him.

His bitterness mounted as he faced the ruin of his hopes. Blindly, erratically his mind stumbled over the events which had led to this. As in a far-off dream he saw the golden house-walls of Rome, the white, dust-laden roads of Italy, the gracious outlines of the crumbling palace of the Apostles where James III, his sad father, held his mock court and lived in phantom

state. Those times seemed almost another life, in some respects
a dreary one for himself and his brother Henry, were it not
for the gleam of gold lightening each of the eventless days, the
dazzle of a crown. From a toddling baby Charles was taught
to look upon the throne of Great Britain as his by right. The
reigning house were usurpers, a cuckoo breed who had no
title and no claims as set against those of the Stuarts. His
thoughts glanced impatiently aside from his childish years
when strange men, bearing English or Scottish names, came to
the mimic court and hailed him as Prince of Wales. All his
heart was set upon the future when he should assume the
position. Nothing else mattered. He bent his mind, narrowly,
stubbornly, to the one aim. He must and should reign as a
king.

His blood ran swiftly, hotly, and his healthy body craved
for action. The constant atmosphere of melancholy, of futile
plotting, of endless letters, in cypher or otherwise, of deferred
hope irked and thwarted him. They were so cautions, these
old, slow-blooded men. His father, prayerful, fearful, expected
little for himself, but Charles was young, strong, determined, and at last the gates swung apart——

They had not been wholly dreary, those days in Rome
which now seemed a lifetime away. He had had Henry's com-
panionship and the unquenchable hope. Sport, dancing,
music—he tasted them all, but in secret he schooled his hardy
frame for greater tasks than passing the idle hours. Lessons?
He laughed and shrugged his shoulders. At fourteen he was
out of the hands of his governors. His mouth twisted sourly as
he remembered them; the Chevalier Ramsay, scholarly, over-
conscientious, whom cabals and intrigues drove from the little
court; Murray, later created Lord Dunbar; and Sheridan, his
left-handed cousin, but the only one whose affection was disinterested and sincere. Charles grinned at haphazard memories
of his youthful rudeness to his tutors. James's grave displeasure and rebukes, and the irking and impatience he felt
after brief spells of travel and enjoyment when the old palace,
moth-eaten, dismal, received him once more—how far-off these
were this April night.

He hated Rome, priest-ridden, dull, where he had no
position, no outlet for his ambitions, and little to absorb his
abounding energies. It was all very well for his father to
preach patience and resignation, and for those around him
to hint that the future held great things. For the present he
might be young, but youth, golden, lovely, did not last for

ever. He was twenty, then twenty-one, finally twenty-two. The years were slipping past, in one sense so dragging and uneventful, in another all too brief for what he longed to accomplish, and he would be old—old, with little to look back upon and no future worth the name.

In winter he had walked on bare feet through snowy woods to toughen his powers of resistance, and he was a fine shot, an excellent horseman, a deft angler. It could not be for nothing that Nature had given him such a constitution, such superb health, a frame which had withstood the rigours of this Scottish campaign and climate. Was he doomed to fail after the great blow struck by his own daring? And failure meant——
A shudder shook him. Capture? Imprisonment? Death? Well, better any one of these alternatives than to return ignominiously to France, to skulk about the Continent, an unwilling pensioner on the bounty of Louis or the Pope, his youth wasted, his sword rusting, his people, who had trusted him, ruined. *Mon Dieu! Mon Dieu!* why has Thou forsaken me?

At one time all had seemed so fair. He recalled the prim face of the courier who carried the French king's letter, summoning him, Charles Edward Stuart, to Paris. His pulses bounded. At last the door of the gilt and cushioned cage which had prisoned his virile young body for twenty-three years was swinging ajar. He had no regrets, no apprehensions, nothing but soaring hopes, youth and high adventure before him. It cost no pang to part with James or Henry.

From the very start he had had to walk warily, staging a mock hunting-party in order to leave Rome unknown to the spies and informers ever alert to watch those of the exiled house and report every movement to Whitehall. It had been in the dead of night on 9th January, 1744, when he slipped from his bed, leaving Henry sleeping soundly, and descended through the ghostly palace to the portico. The wind was keen in his face as he opened the great door to discern a post-chaise, and two saddle-horses, and my Lord Dunbar, who was in the secret, waiting. Ah! that wild drive through the dark along the Albano road. He could scarcely realize that he was free of bonds and restrictions, a man, no longer a boy, with adventures ahead of him, pitfalls and perils innumerable perhaps, but beyond all the glamour of a throne. He ignored cold, danger, the hazard of being recognized and most probably flung into prison. His identity was hidden under the disguise of an officer in the Spanish army, two servants and his father's agent, Balhaldie, who accompanied him, alone being aware of the truth. There were set-backs and delays, a day and night spent at Genoa recuperating from the fatigue and exposure which had exhausted even his iron frame, the voyage from Savona to Antibes, running the gauntlet of a British fleet, and six weary days while the vessel lay in quarantine and he chafed and fretted against the maddening inaction. On a snowy January evening he rode into Paris on horseback, confident, eager, resolved. The French king had not sent for him without some definite purpose.

A fortnight slid past, during which he stayed under the roof of Lord Sempill, a Scot by birth, a Frenchman by environment and inclination. Here the old atmosphere of conspiracy and secrecy, of furtive whispering and concocted plot enveloped him afresh. There were sly visits from men inclined to his Cause, and conferences with the Earl Marischal. Charles scowled. The Marischal had never approved of him. He declared that the Jacobite court at Rome was no place for an honest man and retired to Spain and later Avignon. Now he was glum, foreboding, totally in the dark as to what the French ministers would do for the Prince, ripe to disapprove of every scheme which Charles proposed, and counselling the things Charles hated, patience, waiting, calm.

Invasion was in the air. Everywhere whispers of it crept from mouth to mouth. The war of the Austrian succession was raging. A great fleet lay in readiness at Dunkirk. The English were poorly prepared. Oh, it must succeed, this splendid hazard! He recalled fretting secretly at the way the French king ignored him. He was given no audience, received no invitation to present himself at court, had been told nothing of the part he might play in the expected expedition. Early in February he left Paris, attended by Balhaldie, and travelled to the coast. The little fishing town of Gravelines gave him a lodging, and day after day he stared across the water towards the white cliffs of England over which he intended to rule as king at no distant date.

Fate was cruel. All along he had been tricked, deceived, exploited, used as a pawn to be moved to and fro on Europe's vast political chessboard, but his own hopes, ambitions, agonies and desires were nothing to the men who swayed the pawns. Not human agency alone thwarted him. A higher power—Destiny? Providence? Call it what you will—struck a deeper blow. A great tempest arose, scattering the waiting fleet, and burying Charles's hopes for the time beneath the waves which sank so many of the frail craft. Even now the memory of that terrible night haunted him. The wind howled and raged, the sea was lashed to an incredible height, and the vessel in which he and Marshal Saxe had embarked only reached Dunkirk with the utmost difficulty. Everywhere lay wreckage, torn sails, drowned bodies, wasted equipment. There was nothing for him to do except return to Gravelines and await a further expedition.

The weeks dragged past. Save for Balhaldie, he was alone and almost penniless in a poor lodging, living a furtive, skulking existence, bargaining for fish, carrying home his own purchases, writing lengthy letters to his father or the Earl Marischal (an occupation he hated), his gaze ever fixed on Paris. The French king must send for him, must help him towards his ambition. At his earnest entreaty Sir Thomas Sheridan joined him. Poor Sherry! Charles's mouth was rueful. His success had meant so much to the faithful Irishman.

Ice on the cobbles at Gravelines and a piercing wind. Was it colder than this night, this bleak Scottish spring? The town was small, dreary, the beach a flat, depressing expanse, scourged by perpetual winds. A grey sea, shrouded in mist, hid his longed-for kingdom from his eyes.

He had returned to Paris. A château outside the city was lent to him, and he lived quietly, not without dignity, but, his mind argued feverishly, this stagnation was not life. He yearned to lead, to command, to head an army, to deal in statecraft, politics, empire building. England? Scotland? Ireland? Where had he friends who would lend their swords? The French ministers were wordy and evasive. The French king continued to ignore him, and Charles gritted his teeth as he realized that he was dependent on Louis's capricious bounty. Louis gave him three thousand crowns a month and had paid thirty thousand crowns towards his debts. Charles's mouth tightened. He had a pretty taste in finery and knew well how to enhance his distinguished appearance. The Earl Marischal stressed prudence—always prudence. With a sarcastic brow and a few stinging words he turned aside Charles's eager project of hiring a fishing-boat and embarking for Scotland, where, he averred, many would espouse his Cause.

The Jacobite agents, the wild plots and plans, the stealthy interviews with those dispatched by men working secretly in Scotland for the Jacobite interest. How endless, how futile were the discussions, how empty the promises or suggestions

conveyed in innumerable cipher letters or passed from hand
to hand! He shrugged his shoulders at the recollection of the
Duke of Perth's emissary, John Blaw of Castlehill, a grim-
visaged Lowlander, middle-aged, untravelled, who had come
to him at Candlemas of 1745. Charles had fumbled his way
cautiously during the ensuing conversations. After the faded
ceremony of the palace at Rome, the smooth-spoken, silken
courtesies of the French king's ministers, he found this Scot,
speaking the broad dialect of his native county, the laird of a
small, poverty-stricken estate, blunt, casual, a curious contrast. Sir Hector MacLean, hot for the Cause, son of a father
who had fought at Killiecrankie and Sheriffmuir, had scented
Blaw's arrival and wrote word that D'Argenson wanted to see
him. Charles's hopes soared high. D'Argenson was at the time
Foreign Minister and brother to the Secretary of State for War.
Did this mean that Louis was moving at last on his (Charles's)
behalf? Eagerly he desired Blaw to go and acquaint him on his
return with what had passed. The Prince frowned and pouted.
Lord Sempill engineered the interview. It was vague and
unsatisfactory. Blaw did not see the King. If His Most
Christian Majesty declined to receive Prince Charles Edward
Stuart in audience he was unlikely to grant such a privilege
to any of his emissaries. *Hélas!* Nevertheless, the King was in
the next room. During the hour's interview with D'Argenson,
Lord Sempill demanded in James's name ten thousand
soldiers for England, and Blaw was asked how many were
wanted. Charles's head had lifted proudly as he heard Blaw's
reply. "If the above number was sent to England, Scotland
could do their own affairs themselves, but if there were two
thousand or three thousand to spare we should take them. If
not, we could do without them." The answer—Charles's lip
curled—was that if the demand had been made two months
sooner they could have got them, but that at present there was
not one regiment in France which had not their operations
assigned them for the ensuing campaign. Blaw had been blunt
and plain. He told D'Argenson that he was shortly to set
out again for Scotland and wanted to know what he should
say to the King his master's friends after his return how
far His Most Christian Majesty would go in that affair.
D'Argenson retreated into the adjoining apartment where
King Louis obviously was, and when he emerged directed his
discourse to the Scot. Blaw might assure King James's friends
in Scotland that he would give the men demanded against the
month of October next if the campaign was in any way suc-

cessful in France. How successful Fontenoy and other triumphs revealed, but Charles had not waited until October. That month of dimming mists and driven leaves saw him installed at Holyrood, and Blaw, arrested in Edinburgh with MacLean, now languished in the Tower. MacLean's incarceration proved a grievous blow to the Jacobite interest. He was to have gone to the Highlands and stirred up the wasps' byke of conspiracy and negotiation.

"If he knew his presence unaided would be useful in England he would cross in an open boat." Thus had Charles spoken to vain ears. It had been a mad scheme, this sailing for the Highlands and flinging himself on the mercy of the Scots. Now he saw his naked folly, but at the time it offered the only road of escape from his intolerable situation. He could no longer endure the trickeries, the false promises, the nebulous hopes held out by France. His own agents, quarrelling and intriguing amongst themselves, had deceived him. Murray of Broughton visited him, telling him of those pledged to follow should he lead. Ah! his uneasy conscience reminded him, but Murray only promised that the Scots would support a rising if he brought with him a sufficient army, money, and equipment. He had brought nothing save a small store of both the latter, and so far from being accompanied by French troops, only his seven followers—a motley little group—stood by him. He had refused to see the difficulties, the dangers, the bitter likelihood of defeat, disaster, ignominious return. If he did not conquer he must fall speedily. The hazard was a mad one, but at first it had all the glow and halo of succeeding.

His face softened as he recalled haphazard incidents of the voyage. He had worn as a disguise the dress of a student of the Scots college at Paris and allowed his beard to grow. Sheridan was supposed to be his father. The others—the Duke of Atholl, Sir John MacDonald, Colonel Strickland, now dead at Carlisle, O'Sullivan, Kelly, and Aeneas MacDonald—joined him on board the *Doutelle* at Nantes. To finance the scheme he had borrowed heavily from Waters, the Paris banker, and spent the money recklessly on *fusees*, broadswords, powder, dirks, brandy, small field-pieces, and carried what remained over in a little chest. There had been his first taste of danger when a British man-of-war, the *Lion*, attacked his escorting ship, the *Elizabeth*, and he watched the ensuing fight with quick breath and shining eyes. Waters, his captain, was blunt and uncourtly. He refused to listen to any advice and threat-

ened to send his Royal Highness down to his cabin if he
interfered. Both warring vessels crippled, the *Doutelle* sailed
on alone until the coast of Scotland loomed ahead. Again he
felt the warm, wet winds of Morar, drenched with peat reek,
and saw the sands, gleaming with dazzling whiteness, against
the edge of the blue Atlantic. The floor of a little cave where
he had slept one night was carpeted with white sand. Eriska,
and smoke clouding the low, mean hut in which he and his
friends had passed the first night on Scottish soil. MacDonald
of Boisdale coming next day to his summons and his blunt
advice to the Prince to return home. Charles could hear his
answer, ringing out passionately. "I am come home, sir, and
I will entertain no notion at all of returning to the place
from whence I came, for I am persuaded my faithful Highlanders will stand by me." His companions had echoed Boisdale, imploring him to abandon his project. Cowards!
Poltroons! Faint-hearts! Ignoring them, he had given orders
for the ship to proceed to the mainland, his mind set obstinately on pressing forward. The strange, wild scenery, the
eerie, melancholy crying of sea-birds, the huge, overwhelming
mountains, smoky mist half hiding their bald crowns—all
these had awed him, clouding his high spirits, overshadowing
his hopes. He was doomed to failure. He read this in the
watching faces around him, and when he summoned those on
whose his strongest reliance was set the same excuse, the same
advice fell from every lip. The time was not ripe for a rising.
In coming without substantial support he had failed to keep
his pledge, thus absolving the chiefs from theirs. His cheek
burned as he recalled how he had abased himself, trampling
pride under foot, pleading to Clanranald, Kinlochmoidart,
Lochiel, and others. In the end he had won, and they agreed
to draw their swords for him, but their hearts were not in the
enterprise as his was. All along they had foreseen this inevitable end. Was it the end? He rode faster.

All Scotland had not received him warmly. The Lowlands,
particularly Ayrshire, which did not send him a single
adherent, the bonnet-lairds, the rich merchants, and the crafts-
men in the small burghs, the tenant farmers, above all, the
ministers of the kirks—these had shown no disposition to
welcome him. They were fearful lest their precarious
prosperity should be swallowed up in the maelstrom of another
rising. The old specious argument reared an angry head. Did
not he risk more than they? His life was at stake, his proud
neck forfeit if he failed. What did the loss of a croft, a High-

land estate, a youthful career matter set against all he had to lose?

Glenfinnan! He saw the narrow, craggy vale between its towering mountains where he had set up the royal standard. They had cheered him then, those fierce Highlanders, and followed him blindly. The days were one swift pageant. He pressed downwards through the heart of Scotland, gathering support as he marched. Invergarry! He must make for it again should this night's enterprise fail and Cumberland defeat him. Once more its vast outlines reared before his tired eyes against the last rose of a glowing sunset, and he saw the face of young Angus MacDonell welcoming his Prince. The lad was dust now in Falkirk. Did he bring death and ruin upon all who followed the Stuart star? At the MacDonell stronghold they gathered round him, Lochgarry, Stuart of Appin, young Scotus, Barrisdale, and that sly-eyed messenger from Lord Lovat, Fraser of Gortuleg. He had proffered Lord Lovat's advice, but even then accustomed to treachery and slippery dealing Charles had mistrusted it and preferred to march towards the Atholl country. It had been full summer, with a hint of autumn in the scarlet hips and high, ripe corn. The hot, still air was busy with insect life. He rode into Perth, laughing, and jingling the solitary guinea which was his sole worldly wealth. His heart was high, for he had come home.

Perth proved the rallying-point for more support. Great names had flocked to his standard: the Duke of Perth, Lord Ogilvy, Oliphant of Gask, Lord Strathallan, the Chevalier Johnstone, and many country gentlemen, but chief of all Lord George Murray. Lord George! The Prince frowned deeply. How true were Murray of Broughton's hints and furtive insinuations? Was Lord George in truth treacherous, dangerous, self-seeking? He had been mighty friendly with his Whig brother. At the recent siege of Blair Castle it was rumoured that he failed to take it because he wished to spare a family seat. Charles had loved Blair, with its noble policies, its bowling-green, and its pineapples. He saw himself on his first visit there, the centre of a laughing circle of ladies, watching whilst he bit cautiously into the strange fruit. Their bright eyes and flushed cheeks meant little to him. The Rising was a man's business and a throne the stake. When he visited Blair again he was, whether he himself acknowledged it or not, retreating a second time, but he had striven to seem gay, hunting and hawking, although his heart was broken——

Edinburgh! Here, at least, he had tasted the wine of his highest triumph and been a king. Parts of the city frowned upon him, notably the castle, but at Holyrood his word was law, his orders were obeyed, and more and more support came in. Cope was beaten and the Hanoverian army, fleeing towards Berwick, a laughing-stock. Then it had seemed as though Fortune smiled upon him and the great venture must succeed. He saw the dark council chamber at Holyrood, with its hum of city life outside the old palace, and the faces round the table. The Duke of Perth, thin, eager, delicate; Lord Lewis Gordon, young, ardent, flushed; Lord George, dour, determined, always, Charles reflected, opposed to him, his plans, his schemes, his ideas; Lord Elcho and Lord Ogilvy, alike youthful, gay, sanguine; Lord Nairne, cautious Scot; the great chiefs—Lochiel, Keppoch, Clanranald, Glencoe, Lochgarry, Ardshiel, Glenbucket, stout old veteran, who had arisen from a three years' sick-bed to join his Prince; Sheridan, O'Sullivan, Irish, voluble, hotly at variance with the Scots, and Murray of Broughton, deft, efficient, seldom espousing either side, but a silent, enigmatic personality who always counted. If—if he were to fail, what would be the fate of these men?

He flung up his head defiantly. He must not, should not, fail.

The triple crown dazzled his eyes. Save for the castles of Edinburgh and Stirling, and a few unimportant forts, he had conquered Scotland. The Scots were satisfied and only anxious that he should remain amongst the shadowy pageantry of Holyrood, annul the detested Union, and gather sufficient strength to oppose any force sent against him, but his own ambition rode higher. England beckoned. Once he was over the Border surely the English Jacobites must rise? So he had argued and pleaded with his council, beating down appeal and counter-argument, stressing his eagerness to meet the unprepared Wade. It had been policy, diplomacy to fall in with Lord George's strategy for the march, but he, Charles, had won his way over the greater issue. His mind travelled back to the last night in Edinburgh—Hallowe'en, the Scots called it—when he had slept at Pinkie House, only a few miles from the field where his Highlanders had routed Cope. The smoky sunset, the dim October evening closing in, Hallowe'en revels behind shut doors, the dour satisfaction of the Whig element at the impending departure of the rebels, the tears in the eyes of the pretty Jacobite women, who had had their last glimpse of the young adventurer. At Holyrood all had been bustle and confusion, with the arrival of last-minute recruits, the march out, bagpipes playing and colours flying——

The advance into England seemed blurred, unreal now. Even his reception in the Border counties had foreshadowed failure. None of the old Border families sent their sons to join their lawful Prince. True that at Jedburgh there was discernible a faint under-current of loyalty and enthusiasm. A rabble of eager boys in their 'teens ran out of the town to meet the Highlanders approaching from Kelso, and walked alongside him, goggle-eyed, as he entered the town by the Canongate bridge. One Walter Scott, a weaver, mounted on the parapet, greeted him with the salutation, "God prosper Prince Charles, our lawful King." The Provost was a Whig. At an open space of the burgh he addressed a large gathering of citizens whose sympathies were Hanoverian, but the speech had been rudely interrupted. An old woman's shrill voice called out: "What for is the Callant no' gettin' his ain?" His lips curved in sour amusement at the still unanswered question.

Dusk fell early. The land was sad and dim, misted by the breath of winter. A little glen, known locally as the Black Burn, lay behind the house in the Castlegate where he lodged. During the sodden November afternoon he strolled through its leafless peace and seated himself on a large whinstone which glimmered greyly out of the half-dark. For long he sat there, motionless, brooding over the prospect of his adventure, ere he shook off his mood——

He saw the wintery landscape beyond the Border, small, flat, commonplace, set against the serried mountain-peaks of the Highlands, the long lochs, the brawling rivers, the wide autumn fields. Here grey skies matched the wet roads, the sodden tracks, the bare hedges. The town of Carlisle was the first English city to bar his path to the throne. It was poorly defended by the militia of Cumberland and Westmorland, under the weak-kneed Coldstreamer, Colonel Durrand. The deputy-mayor was a fool. Charles had sent his summons to surrender, which the deputy-mayor refused to obey. The rumour ran that Wade was marching from Newcastle to re-lieve Carlisle. The blockade of the city was begun, the French officers rendering themselves ridiculous by their fulsome praises of Lord George Murray's siege arrangements. It had been intensely cold. He saw Atholl and Perth, regardless of dignity, poor physique, the inclement weather conditions which only the hardy Highlanders could face with equanimity, toiling in the trenches in their shirt-sleeves. Ah! had all those whom he commanded been as unselfish, as loyal, as disinterested he might have sat in St. James's ere this.

After a feeble, futile resistance the town capitulated. Eh! but Edinburgh had taught him a lesson. He had never mastered its castle, that frowning stronghold still housing its Hanoverian garrison. There should be no such error with Carlisle. Town and castle must become his. Ultimately his terms had been agreed to, and—his worn young face flushed— on a November morning he rode into Carlisle, mounted upon a white horse, a hundred pipers striding ahead, blaring their shrill music. During the brief siege, in a dense fog which hid everything, the defenders had heard the bagpipes playing outside the English gate. Strange, sad melody. He loved those wild strains. The town council received him on their knees. The city's keys were handed to him. He showed himself gracious and magnanimous. He could afford to be. It was his first English triumph.

Was it wholly one? At Carlisle the earliest open rupture occurred between himself and Lord George Murray. Charles flushed again, this time angrily. No doubt it had been tactless, ungracious of him to allow the Duke of Perth and Murray of Broughton to arrange the terms of surrender instead of Lord George, but, *mon Dieu!* what an explosion, what unpleasantness, what a vastly disagreeable position he, the Prince Regent, was placed in! His brow darkened as he remembered Lord George's curt letter, resigning his commission, but desiring to serve as a volunteer, and his own indecently hasty acceptance of the offer. Was not he in supreme command, his the deciding voice? *Ma foi!* it did not seem like it. The army muttered and threatened what amounted to mutiny, the chiefs dissented and disapproved, and he, Charles Edward, was forced to pocket his pride, to reinstate Lord George, and to slight the Duke of Perth. *Hé!* Perth had been mighty tactful, declining to supersede Lord George and being content with a subordinate position, the command of his own regiment, but the incident, trifling, ridiculous, did not make for harmony. Sheridan had lectured him, told him plainly that he had been in the wrong and must summit——

The winter grew harder, the cold more searing, his situation more unstable, precarious, and perilous. His army left Carlisle—the name was sour on his tongue—and pressed southwards. There was danger from Wade and his force at Newcastle, and the Duke of Cumberland, fresh from his military service on the Continent, appointed in Ligonier's stead, lay at Lichfield. A rumour arose, too, of an army of ten thousand mustering on Finchley common. The smaller towns —Penrith, Kendal, Lancaster, Preston, and Wigan—did not oppose him, but—— Where were the great English families, the eager Jacobite squires, upon whose support he had so surely reckoned? No message reached him from any important name. No word of an army risen to link with his own was ever brought. Instead, everywhere he saw sullen faces, and rain dripped drearily from eaves and gutters as a hoarse-voiced herald proclaimed King James III and VIII at each weather-worn market-cross in the obscure, squalid towns and hamlets.

England! The country was grey, sour, with a gaping peasantry who watched him ride by, and mean cities full of little shopkeepers who hated his exactions. Did they expect his army to exist on air? He paid in hard coin for everything he ate or drank. They should be glad, proud, these English-men, to acclaim and serve their rightful Prince and send the Hanoverians packing. The drubbing received at Fontenoy ought to have served as a lesson. His heart-beats quickened as he remembered that breathless May day a bare eleven months ago when, lurking outside Paris, an embarrassing, unacknow-ledged guest, he learned of the British defeat and Marshal Saxe's triumph. His own hopes had soared, absurdly, he now realized, for the French king had merely continued to ignore him, driving him, he argued fiercely, to carry out his own secret plans. He saw himself in the private room of the elder Waters, his Paris banker, laughing into the cautious, seamed old face. No, he had no security, except his jewels at Rome, but for our object he would pawn even his shirt. He did not want money for plate or fine clothes or costly entertainment. Here his mirth died. He needed it to buy arms, equipment, brandy, anything required to bolster up this wild expedition. If he did not act now, another opportunity might not come for years. He had coaxed and pleaded, stormed, shed tears, and at length the old man yielded. The money was lent. One day —Charles shrugged his shoulders—King James would pay it back, or he himself, from St. James's, would summon Waters to London to receive his due. Eh, *mon ami?*

Manchester! Here, for the first time, faces wore smiles of welcome, bells rang out, and bonfires blazed in celebration of his entry. It seemed an earnest of the success to come. At two o'clock in the afternoon he arrived, marching on foot, surrounded by a body of Highlanders, himself wearing High-

C

land dress. The day was short, foggy, wintery. Manchester's narrow streets seemed vague, cloudy, with faces like blurs behind the dimly lit windows. Through the thick air sounded the rasping notes of the bellman's summons, "to give notice to all persons belonging to the excise, innkeepers, etc., forthwith to bring their last acquittances and rolls, and all the ready cash they had in their hands belonging to the Government, on pain of military execution." After his own arrival the bellman stumped round the town again, giving orders that the houses were to be illuminated. The lamps and candles glowed feebly in the misty, insubstantial atmosphere. His quarters were in Market Street Lane, the house of a Manchester merchant, one John Dickenson. Charles recalled him now, clad in Quaker-like garments of neutral hues, bewigged, precise, placing his dwelling and all it contained at the service of the Prince Regent, but in his heart hating this Highland intrusion and the exactions it entailed. He remembered a stuffed bird behind glass, solemn books, a dish of apples shrilly red, an old mirror on a faded wall. At dinner he had been gay, confident, laughing with his officers, extolling the number of recruits from Manchester who had espoused his Cause, and initiating a merry dispute as to the manner of his entry into London. Should he wear the Highland or the Lowland dress, and was he to walk or to ride? London—— London. Ah, far, how far? They broke his heart at Derby instead.

He had been avid to go forward, confident in his Highlanders, but his council—plague take them, the cautious cowards!—advised, nay, ordered, retreat at Derby. The shock had half-stunned him. Only the night before he had marched into the town, to be well received. There were bonfires on the roads, bells rang out through the frosty air, the windows were illuminated, and a crowd had followed him as he made his way to his quarters at Exeter House. His hopes were high. Had he not baffled the slow-moving Wade and even Cumberland? London was little less than a hundred and thirty miles away. Retreat to Scotland! Even now, four months afterwards, he could still recall his stark incredulity, his helpless rage, his bewildered pain, his impotence to move these hard Scots. "Rather than go back I would wish to be twenty feet underground!" he had cried. Once again he abased himself before them, this time to no purpose. He blinked back angry tears. The throne had been within his grasp, but he had had to turn his heel upon it and fight his way again to the dreariness and murk of Scotland. The weather was a blurred

tapestry of rain, snow, sleet, and mud-encrusted roads. On the
march south these things had been there merely to be jested at
or laughed away as of small account, but with defeat and
despair as his companions they added to the prevailing
wretchedness. His army, hitherto well conducted and well
behaved, vented its disappointment in plundering. Re-
prisals followed. The Jacobites were obliged to make their
way through a hostile countryside, with an angered peasantry
placing every conceivable obstacle in the path of their retreat.
The county militia harassed them, and beacons were lighted
on hill-tops to warn the neighbourhood of the Young Pretender's approach. Snow lay deep and the temperature was
Arctic. They dared not pause or halt or slacken. Speed—
speed, or their foes would fall upon them——

His face clouded afresh as he recollected the second visit
to Manchester, the anger his demands aroused, the defiant
attitude of the citizens towards his reappearance and his
claims. The town was hostile and unfriendly. It knew that it
had to deal with an army in reverse and a Prince fleeing from
his enemies. About ten thousand of the inhabitants collected, armed with pickaxes to spoil the roads, and carrying
scythes and hedge-stakes, very hearty to have a brush with the
rebels. The indispensable bellman had again to be summoned, this time to order the mob to disperse. Stones were
thrown at the advance guard of the Highlanders. Charles had
signed a warrant demanding five thousand pounds by four
o'clock of the next day. In the grey December morning a group
of long-faced citizens waited upon him. It was, they averred,
impossible to raise the money. He had received them almost
sullenly. The payment could not be excused. After lengthy
argument he consented to reduce the amount to half, but this,
he declared, must be levied on Manchester and Salford by
one o'clock. They had gone out, heads hanging, lips muttering, and he lingered, moody, depressed, until a commotion
outside the door aroused him. Four Highlanders had seized
an inoffensive citizen, one James Bailey, and brought him to
Murray of Broughton at Mr. Dickenson's, where Charles was
again lodged. They threatened to keep him a prisoner until
the money was paid, or, if it were not, to carry him off with
the army as a hostage. Mr. Bailey protested that he was
between seventy and eighty years of age, had not slept out of
his own bed for two years, "nor could bear to travel." He was
told that if unable to ride they would procure a wheel-carriage
for his use. Charles peeped out and saw him, a small, mole-

coloured gnome of a man, gesticulating and objecting feebly. With a shrug of his shoulders the Prince told his secretary to inform Mr. Bailey that his Royal Highness, in consideration of his age, if he would give his word and honour to fetch two thousand, five hundred pounds in two hours, or surrender himself a prisoner, consented that he should have his liberty for so long. Mr. Bailey agreed, with every appearance of thankfulness. From the window, Charles watched him scuttling out of the house and down the dim street. The money was procured and paid by two o'clock. Bah! these rich, mean English!

He had decreed that his army should halt at Manchester for a day, but Lord George instantly vetoed this. The men did not require the rest and the delay would only give the enemy time to advance upon them. Charles had stayed firm, but afterwards he weakened and sent O'Sullivan at two in the morning to tell Lord George that it was decided to march that day. As contrary orders had been given it was eleven o'clock before a start could be made. The wet day's toil along appalling roads resembled a nightmare, the rearguard straggling into the dirty little town called Wigan with the aid of lamps and candles. The Duke of Perth was sent ahead to hasten the reinforcements in Scotland. The country people drove him back ignominiously. Charles gnawed his underlip——

Confusion and quarrels about orders and counter-orders led to delays and set-backs innumerable. That the army reached Scottish soil again more or less intact was, Charles knew, wholly due to the strategy and resource of Lord George Murray, hampered and hindered at every turn by stupidity, obstinacy, or malice. They were in Carlisle again, and though he must march out of the town hurriedly the Prince was reluctant to abandon it, an empty shell for the Whigs to recover. He reddened angrily as he remembered his implacable decision to leave behind a garrison of some three hundred and fifty men. To those who questioned the arrangement he had airy reasons ready. He designed to return one day with the strength gathered in Scotland. It was desirable to keep the Stuart standard floating at some point in England. How Lord George Murray had scowled and then stated bluntly that this was madness. He had offered to remain in the town with the Atholl Brigade, if the Prince commanded, though, he muttered angrily, he knew what his and their fate would be. A safe suggestion, my Lord George. Even the Duke of Perth had objected to leaving any of his men. Charles's smouldering obstinacy was fanned to a steady flame. It had not been his fault, the bitter sequel. How could he have foretold that Carlisle would fall to the Duke of Cumberland and the hapless garrison, surrendering, be reserved for the Elector's pleasure? Did that mean death? He shuddered. At Glasgow, in the midst of his stay in the Whig and hostile city, two who had escaped over the wall stole to him with the tale of Carlisle's capitulation——

The dreadful winter days dragged by. He was across the Esk and once more on Scottish soil. Christmas was spent at Hamilton Palace, a strange day, with hunting in the parks under frozen skies for diversion. The bulk of his army had gone on to Glasgow and he entered the city the following afternoon. Nowhere, he reflected bitterly, had he met with so few friends. On the streets none cheered him or cared to watch him pass. Few women's faces were visible behind windows or at close-mouths, and he learned with sour amazement that those who saw him pronounced him not handsome. He secured a savage satisfaction by fitting out his ragged army at Glasgow's expense and leaving the city early in January to lay siege to Stirling. The town capitulated; the castle did not. He took up his quarters at Bannockburn House, gazing with kindling eyes upon the field won by his famous ancestor. Lord George Murray and Lord John Drummond were at Alloa, making arrangements for the conveyance across the Forth of the cannon brought from Perth. The siege of Stirling Castle dragged on. In Edinburgh the Government troops massed and he learned that Hawley was marching towards Linlithgow and Falkirk. That dark afternoon of wind and rain which saw his second resounding victory over his enemies had advantaged him little in the end. Again the chiefs urged retreat upon him. Again he yielded——

Was the return from Derby a wise course? Day and night the doubt tortured him. Lord George had stressed the manifold desertions amongst his army, the vastly greater forces accumulated against him, the lack of succours in England or from abroad. Now he saw that all along Louis of France had played with him, subtly encouraged him after the die was cast, used him as pawn and puppet for his own ends, but had never intended to support his claims. The little aid the French king had dispatched was negligible, a drop in the bucket, a sop, a mockery. Charles recalled D'Eguilles, that smooth-tongued ambassador, who had arrived at Holyrood in October. He counselled waiting, as the Earl Marischal had done earlier, distrusting any invasion of England, but he had hinted distinctly at help from France by no distant date. Too late! Too late! Foreign ships had been sunk or captured during these last forlorn weeks as the Prince's affairs drew to the climax of this night's mad hazard, and he was penniless, his officers deep in private feuds and quarrels, the Irish everlastingly bickering with the Scots, and a thousand grievances, complaints, or tales of desertion, depredation, and theft being brought perpetually to his own unwilling ear.

The end loomed near—after so much. He could not bring himself to realize or acknowledge it, even in his own sore heart. His men, ill-equipped, unprepared, unaccustomed to warfare, had inflicted two sound defeats on seasoned professional soldiers. Would it not be so again? He thought of the night of Falkirk, the rain beating down on the piled bodies of his dead foes, and the wish visited him that he had followed up this success by advancing upon Edinburgh a second time. Alas! he had been over-persuaded, overruled, and instead had struggled on with the futile siege of Stirling Castle. Then had come the second retreat—forced upon him, as the one at Derby had been, he mused bitterly—the straggling march towards Inverness and the Highlands, and the long days and weeks of waiting. A few small successes cheered him, but always there lurked the knowledge that Cumberland was ready, biding his time, consolidating his forces, nursing his advantage until he deemed it wise to strike. The hour had nearly dawned. His spies knew all—Charles gnawed at his lip, recognizing this—the desertions in the Jacobite camp, the lack of foreign aid, the scattering of a large bulk of available troops in futile operations such as the besieging of Blair Castle and Fort William. Men from Fort William had come in time, abandoning their attempt to take the place, but Cluny MacPherson, guarding the passes, was not yet arrived from Badenoch, and Lord Cromarty and his young son Lord MacLeod were absent in Sutherland. The *Hazard*, the vessel captured so daringly off Montrose in the previous October, returning from France with money and stores, had been chased by English cruisers in the Pentland Firth and forced ashore. Her loss was grievous. The Prince found himself deprived of Murray of Broughton's able services through illness, and on all sides he heard angry grumblings about Hay's mismanagement of the commissariat. His own healthy hunger stressed this. Could his men, foodless, chilled, disheartened, succeed in the night attack? At the time it had seemed the sole chance of avoiding a battle. Even Lord George, who appeared to take a peculiar pleasure in thwarting his Prince, had approved——

Until the Highlanders had assembled for the march. Then, with lengthened visage, he had pointed out how large a number had slipped away in quest of food, and who could blame them? Charles refused to admit this. The men would all return in good heart when the start was made. He had stood there, looking at Lord George's grim, disapproving countenance, the night-wind fluttering his cloak, the cold air from the river in his face. A dank, chilling mist was creeping along the ground, clouding the fires lighted to deceive the enemy into thinking that the rebels were still gathered at Culloden. Others supported Lord George, but he had overruled them, cried the order to march, at the same time embracing Lord George, and as it was a bare hour after sunset, surely Nairn could be reached by two o'clock?

He drew his horse to a standstill as a figure loomed out of the dark. A voice called: "Is that your Royal Highness?" Charles returned a breathless affirmative. He recognized young Anderson of Whitburgh. Memory stirred in him of his pease-straw bed at Gladsmuir and Lord George awakening him to tell him that Anderson, who possessed a good acquaintance with the locality, knew of a way across a bog within a short distance of Cope's left flank where the Highlanders could pass in comparative safety without the enemy's knowledge. This had contributed materially to the swift winning of the battle, and Charles had held the young man in esteem ever afterwards. Now he peered at him through the murk and pallid dark, saying impatiently: "Well? Well?"

"I am the bearer of a message from my Lord George Murray, sir."

The Prince's breath came hard. "What is it?"

"His lordship proposes a retreat either to Culloden House or Inverness."

"A—retreat?"

"Sir, it is unavoidable. Owing to the delay in marching dawn is breaking, and Lord George judges it impossible to make the concerted attack."

"Is this Lord George Murray's opinion alone, Mr. Anderson?"

"No, sir. Others are with him in agreeing that a retreat is imperative."

"*I* cannot agree." Charles's voice was high, furious. "What do we gain by turning back?"

"It will at least afford the men a chance of mustering in full strength, sir. The desertions are excessive. The Camerons alone are half the number."

"What says Lochiel?"

"Does your Royal Highness wish for word with him, sir?"

"At once."

A gaunt Highlander was beckoned from the long, drooping column and sent in quest of the Cameron chief. Charles sat biting his lip.

"I refuse to consent to a retreat." He spoke passionately.

"But, sir——"

"I will hear of nothing save advancing and attacking the enemy. Give my Lord George Murray orders to that purpose."

"At least hear Lochiel first, sir."

"Why should I? I—I, the Prince Regent, command."

Anderson of Whitburgh stayed silent. Although he was outside the jealously guarded circle of those near the Prince's person he had tasted of Charles's autocratic temper and implacable obstinacy. Here was another example of both.

"I cannot understand the delay." Charles's voice was fretful. "We left Culloden soon after sunset."

"The men are fatigued, sir, and started fasting. They cannot move with any speed."

Charles tugged restlessly at his horse's bridle.

"Sir?" Cameron of Lochiel had come up.

The Prince started. "Ha! Lochiel. What is this?"

"Lord George Murray has ordered retreat, sir. There is no other measure possible."

"Lord George? Lord George? But you, Lochiel? You cannot urge that?"

Lochiel's face was pale and distressed, but Charles's heart sank when he saw the look of determination stamped upon it.

"I am with Lord George, sir. I feel most strongly that we should go back. It is not my voice alone. All the officers in the front are for returning."

"No, no, no! Never! Never!" The Prince spoke with such passionate vehemence that even the drowsy ranks of Highlanders, who could not comprehend the English tongue, realized that Tearlach was angered and annoyed. "I am not for going back. Is it not far better to march forward and attack than to march back and be attacked afterwards?"

The veil of darkness was thinning. Behind the trees a paling sky showed and a sleepy bird twittered.

"If my men—to name these only, sir—were their full

strength, it might be advisable, but the desertions are so serious——"

"*Mon Dieu!* am I responsible for those? Must I suffer and my schemes be thwarted because your Camerons leave the ranks?"

" 'Tis not my Camerons alone, sir. At least two thousand men are missing, and that is a vast number."

Charles's speech was hoarse and broken. "They were famished, Lochiel. Can any be blamed for stealing away in search of food?"

The Prince's quick generosity touched Lochiel. "You are hungry, too, sir."

"So are we all, but we stay at our posts. We cannot retreat."

"I fear the return march has already begun, sir."

"Against my orders? My express orders?"

"You Royal Highness was a mile back and there was not time to send a message and await your answer."

"Which would have been a refusal. But——"

His words broke off as he realized that there was a movement amongst the huddled column. Men were trickling slowly towards him, their faces set in the direction from whence they had come. He asked hoarsely where they were going. The answer came: "We are ordered by the Duke of Perth to return to Culloden House."

Charles sat shaken with fury. "Where is the Duke of Perth? Call him here. Ah! Perth. What do you mean by ordering the men back?"

"Lord George Murray, sir, with the first column, has gone three-quarters of an hour ago."

"Good God! What can be the matter? What does he mean? We were equal in number, and would have blown them to the devil. Pray, Perth, cannot you call them back yet? Perhaps he is not gone far."

"I regret, sir, Lord George is already so far on his way back that it would be impossible to bring up the army in time enough to execute the intended plan."

Hotly the Prince argued. Quietly the Duke of Perth stated and stressed the position. In the end Charles muttered sullenly: " 'Tis no matter, then. We shall meet them like brave fellows. There is no help for it, my lads. March back to Culloden House."

CHAPTER IV

LORD ELCHO WAS WITH HIS LIFEGUARDS. HE HAPPENED TO BE
as hungry, as disillusioned, as apprehensive as anybody else
who understood the position, but he still contrived to look
debonair, carefree, and spruce. The chief feeling in his mind
was regret, mingled with disgust at his own incredible folly
in throwing in his lot with this mad adventure of the Rising.
He was young, somewhere about the Prince's own age, and
youth believed that anything might happen. At twenty-four
he had already drunk deeply from the goblet of life. Travel,
adventure, London, Edinburgh, the Grand Tour—my Lord
Elcho, eldest son and heir of the Earl of Wemyss, had enjoyed
all these. Before him there had stretched an agreeable prospect
of fulfilling the easy duties of his position, marrying suitably,
begetting children, and dying in his bed, respected, esteemed,
full of years, but—— His was an impatient, active temperament. He had forsaken the safe, dull highway mapped out for
him, however gilded by the fashionable follies of the eighteenth
century, and chose instead uncharted country which now
proved a bog, a quagmire, a maze of sinking sands. Politics
lured him, and his family had always inclined to the Stuarts.
Like Hay of Restalrig, he could not plead ignorance. He had
known perfectly well what was in the wind——

All his life, he reflected impatiently, there had been talk
of another rising in favour of the exiled Stuarts. The 'Fifteen
had proved a dismal, uninspired failure under Mar's leader-
ship, but the flame still burned. Men visited the Continent,
ostensibly for enjoyment and experience, or, if they had young
sons, these were dispatched abroad by way of completing their
education. Such travels invariably embraced a stay in Rome
and a private audience of the Chevalier de St. George, as the
polite styled King James. My Lord Elcho himself had had this
privilege. His lip curled a little at the memory. Secrecy,
mystery, false names, furtive entry by private door and concealed stair. It seemed impossible to gain access to the tiny
exiled court without these trappings. James had made a
nebulous, vaguely agreeable impression upon Elcho's memory,
a dim picture of melancholy graciousness, of a man who had
suffered so many disappointments, set-backs, rebuffs, that in
time he ceased to harbour any hopes for himself. His worn-

out, repeatedly frustrated ambitions were now centred in his sons, notably the elder.

Charles Edward Stuart! Elcho looked back over the slight intercourse he had had with Charles at Rome. The Prince impressed him chiefly by his prowess in sport and his amazing bodily endurance. He had been born for war, and even the hardships and austerities of the present campaign, the violent contrast between Italy's burning heat and the savage cold of Scotland had only affected his health temporarily a few weeks previously. He could march for miles at the head of his High-landers, eat anything, endure wind, sleet, rain, snow, lack of sleep, and even of the ordinary comforts of civilization. What a king he would make, his admirers whispered, but Elcho, a little scornful, had wondered in Rome how much lay behind that glowing exterior. Had the Prince the wits to challenge experienced adversaries, the skill to play a lone hand without dependence upon others who were out for their own gain? In some ways he was a fool, my Lord Elcho reflected. He lent too ready an ear to the counsel of those who sided with his own inclinations. A rabble of landless Irish and needy Scots had surrounded him from the first. If he had trusted Lord George Murray, instead of imbibing the poison of tales and untruths about him, his affairs might have prospered better. And yet—— What chance of success had the reckless, mismanaged rising, with no foreign support?

Elcho recalled Paris in the winterly January of 1744. It was cold, the rime sparkling on the cobbles, as he went to pay his duty to the Prince who had come to the French capital on King Louis's invitation. The house where he lodged was inconspicuous. Lord Elcho remembered moss-grown steps leading down to an old well in the courtyard and a leafless poplar against a wall. The Prince seemed unusually nervous. Hitherto Elcho had always known him sanguine, eager, impul-sive, inclined to rashness. The talk was all of the proposed French expedition against England. Charles was to sail with Marshal Saxe and Elcho must lend his sword. A little wearied by the gaieties of Paris, despite the rigours of war, he had acquiesced, but when the storm wrecked Charles's hopes, Elcho once more embarked on foreign travel. The Jacobite Cause, despite its recent set-back, was not dead. He met Murray of Broughton on business connected with a rising and often wondered how far Murray's encouragement had led the Prince to take the mad step of landing, alone and unsupported, on Scottish soil.

He remembered his own dismay when the news reached him. It had been a close, stifling August day, and the mingled smells of Edinburgh in summer had drifted up to the high *land* where Elcho lodged. A letter from Buchanan of Arnprior carried the fatal information. The Prince had disembarked on the west coast of Scotland. Elcho had gone to his home, Wemyss Castle, and loitered there whilst stories of the strength and gains of the expedition grew daily. It was succeeding beyond expectation, more certainly than the most sanguine hopes had pictured. The Highland army was advancing unopposed upon Edinburgh. Elcho's doubts dissolved like mist in the sunshine of the Prince's enterprise. He rode to join him and he did not come penniless. Fifteen hundred golden guineas jingled in a bag by his saddle. At this juncture—he grinned sourly—he seemed unlikely ever to handle a penny of the money again.

It was September. The cornfields spread a motionless golden tapestry, for there was no wind. The Prince had his quarters at Gray's Mill, a little ugly stone house four miles from Edinburgh, overlooking a sluggish river. The surrounding fields were flat and ill-drained. Trees, their green slowly turning to bronze and brown and saffron, stood sentinel against the long outline of the Pentland hills. A lighted window made a square of yellow. The low-browed room, little bigger than a cupboard, where the Prince held his court, was a haze of tobacco smoke and a blur of half-remembered faces. Charles was changed, a man, he who had been the restless youth of Rome, Paris, and Gravelines. Elcho noted an increased hauteur, a further dignity, an air of authority and command absent hitherto. The Prince showed himself very gracious, instantly offering Elcho the position of his Royal Highness's chief aide-de-camp, and jestingly stressing his poverty as a reason for not refusing the proffered gold. He had, he avowed gaily, only fifty guineas in his possession.

The voice of the mill-stream was loud through the quiet. A coach lumbered up, bringing the deputies from Edinburgh to plead with the Prince in response to his demand for the city's surrender.

Elcho had been alone with Charles. Scarcely did the ill-fitting door shut upon the rest when the Prince began to speak, volubly, eagerly, of Lord George Murray. Lord George, he averred, had only joined him in order to betray him. Elcho's raised eyebrows and involuntary head-shake merely drove Charles to renewed vehemence. It was true, *true*.

"But, sir——"

"You do not know the circumstances." The light, high voice grew rasping, breathless. "My Lord George is brother to the Whig who styles himself Duke of Atholl."

"And also, sir, to Duke William, who accompanied your Royal Highness from France."

"I know I know. But, *mon cher,* listen. Directly Duke James (I call him so from courtesy) heard of my arrival in Scotland and learned that the Highlands were rising to support their lawful Prince, he appointed Lord George a sheriff-deputy (oh! your Scots terms. I cannot yet bring my tongue round some of them, for all my Scotch blood) for Perthshire."

"Surely he does not hold that office now, sir?"

"No, no. But when Sir John Cope—— There is no one listening?"

"Shall I ascertain, sir?"

The Prince nodded. Elcho tiptoed to the door and flung it open with abrupt suddenness. Only an empty strip of dusty passage, with a spider's-web high up on the wall, and at the end the motionless figure of a Highland sentry, was to be seen.

"Your Royal Highness is entirely private, sir."

"Good! Well, this Cope went northward from Edinburgh and halted at Crieff. There he held an interview with Duke James, and Duke James's brother, my Lord George Murray, was present."

At the Prince's nod of permission, Elcho had resumed his seat. He sat frowning. Charles, he was aware, watched him narrowly.

"May I ask, sir, how your Royal Highness obtained this information?"

The haughty brows rose. "That is of no moment. It is true."

"I do not doubt that, sir, but much depends on who carried it to your ear."

Charles broke out pettishly: "As I have said, my Lord Elcho, that is not of any moment. What matters is that Lord George Murray, who joined me at Perth, and whom I appointed lieutenant-general of my forces, who gave me every assurance of his loyalty to my person and the Cause, now proves to have been leagued with my enemies but a short while before. I do not trust him. I should not."

Elcho remonstrated firmly. "Has he given your Royal Highness reason to doubt his fidelity or his motives?"

Charles reiterated stubbornly: "I do not trust him. White-hall has set a price upon my head. He could earn it by a word."

There was a grim little silence. Both young men, only twenty-four, though one was a prince, saw the bewigged heads in London bent over the document they were drawing up, offering thirty thousand pounds to any person who should seize and secure the elder son of the Pretender. It was a vast sum, wealth for an individual, a fortune for a clan. Elcho's breath came hard. Hitherto he had failed to realize the gravity and uncertainty of Charles's position, the hourly peril in which he stood, day or night. If he landed anywhere in Great Britain or Ireland, or was found on board any vessel with intent to land, then a myriad hands might seize him, secure him, and give him over to the Government. Not all, even amongst his own party, were staunch. However guarded, however cherished, no matter how careful, he was never safe from his foes. Was his fear of Lord George justified, and did he indeed believe that the latter had only offered his sword to the Cause from the basest motives, and was biding his opportunity to betray his Prince?

Elcho stammered stupidly: "But Lord George Murray's record, sir? He was 'out' in '15 and again in '19, and exiled for years because of his activities in both risings."

"Yet he accepted a pardon from the Government." Charles's voice grated.

"And during the time, sir, until your Royal Highness's landing, how was he occupied?"

The Prince shrugged his shoulders in the foreign fashion which so often emphasized his words.

"He played the country gentleman, my lord. He has an estate in Perthshire—Tullibardine—where I dined on my way southward. He married, and his family are growing up. That is another thing. His eldest son is much with his Whig uncle who has bought him a commission in Lord Loudoun's regiment."

"A boy of his age, sir! What do his opinions on politics matter?"

"Mighty little, yet I was told that he took very ill his father's coming out."

Elcho stayed discreetly silent.

"No, I cannot trust Lord George," Charles repeated. "I fear. I fear——"

His fire and impatience died. He relapsed into a brooding melancholy and quiet which, to Elcho's mind, emphasized his likeness to his father. The younger man sat thinking, puzzling, weighing facts against each other. If he could learn who had brought this tale of Lord George to Charles's ear——

"Your Royal Highness has many adherents whose politics and loyalty might be as much suspect as Lord George Murray's, sir," he murmured at length.

"*Comment?* Such as——?"

"MacPherson of Cluny, sir, for one."

Charles's frown deepened.

"Cluny? You seem to forget, my lord, that he is in Badenoch, raising his clan for my Cause."

"I am aware, sir, that Cluny has joined your Royal Highness, but before espousing the winning side"—Elcho copied the Prince's foreign gesture of shrugged shoulders—"was his conduct any more creditable than that of my Lord George Murray?"

Charles was flushed and scowling. Elcho saw that his arrow had sped between the joints of the royal harness. Early in August, Cluny had declared openly for the Government and the previous June he had accepted a commission as captain in Lord Loudoun's Highland regiment. Nay, more, he was even raising men for the Elector when Lochiel and his Camerons took him prisoner and carried him to the Prince at Dalwhinny. His *volte face* had followed a supposed insult from Cope, but why should the Prince believe in Cluny's change of front and politics and mistrust Lord George's similar action?

"Cluny is our friend," snapped the Prince.

"But surely, sir, Lord George has shown no signs of being other than loyal?"

"Murray thought——" The Prince caught himself up, yet not before the name had given Elcho the clue he sought.

"Was it Mr. Murray of Broughton who carried to your Royal Highness this tale of Lord George's interview with Cope at Crieff, sir?"

"I repeat that it is no matter who told me, my lord, when it is true."

Elcho had had a glimpse of the Prince's implacable obstinacy, an obstinacy, he now realized, which had gone far to wreck the campaign. Charles's partiality for the Irish, smooth-spoken and incapable, his stubborn decisions such as the fatal one of leaving a garrison at Carlisle, his refusal to hold any more councils after the final one at Derby that had blighted his glowing hopes—all these were indications of a soured temper, a distrustful outlook, and a mind warped by disappointment and frustrated ambition. Even as early as the evening at Gray's Mill, Elcho saw that his young leader would prove difficult to handle. He said smoothly:

"What chanced between Sir John Cope and Cluny Mac-Pherson, sir?"

Charles recovered his temper and laughed.

"Oh, a bonny clash between English stupidity and High-land pride, I believe. Lochiel can give you the details better than I. Cluny vowed that Sir John did not understand how to treat a gentleman, a Highland chief, and an angel could not resist the soothing close applications of the rebels."

"So your Royal Highness trusts him?"

"Why should I not?" Charles's chin tilted haughtily. "He and Murray of Broughton worked together for the Cause long ere I landed."

"But Lord George, sir—— Was that a knock?"

At the Prince's sign Elcho went to open the door. Four of the Town Council were without, asking for an audience of his Royal Highness. They were bidden to enter and a quartet of fat bailies obeyed. However much it went against the grain each kissed the Prince's hand. Charles smiled upon them with narrowed eyes. "Well, gentlemen?" he asked.

"We are here, sir, to implore your Royal Highness to give us time to think over your demands," quavered the fattest.

"I can grant no time."

The bailies' faces fell. Elcho, standing back discreetly in the shadows, saw their plan. As he rode towards Edinburgh the talk everywhere had been of a landing by General Cope, on his way from Aberdeen, at Leith. To delay, to temporize, was the authorities' object, as if Cope came in time a battle between his forces and the Highland army was inevitable and might save the capital. There were murmured remonstrances and appeals. The Prince's face hardened.

"I can grant no time." The repetition came curtly. "I am going to send a detachment to attack the town, and let you defend it at your peril."

"Eh, sir!" quavered the oldest bailie.

"If you do, the consequences will be bad." Charles was no longer smiling. "If you do not, I intend no harm to the ancient metropolis of my kingdom."

The deputation bundled out in undignified haste. The Prince then summoned his officers and ordered Lochiel with eight hundred men to march and attack the city. After they had gone everything was held in an atmosphere of unease and apprehension. What would follow? Had Cope already

landed? The latter supposition seemed unlikely as a further
deputation of six counsellors came out from Edinburgh,
headed by a former provost, and made the same request for
delay as the first. They received a similar answer, delivered
through a third party. Charles declined to see them.

The night was very still. The Prince moved restlessly about
the narrow room. Elcho watched him in silence. His own
blood ran swiftly. By this time to-morrow was that slender,
erect figure to be master of Scotland, installed in the sunken
palace which had witnessed the triumphs and tragedies of so
many of his fated house, or would he be defeated, fugitive, or
prisoner? *Thirty thousand pounds for the person of the Pretender's elder son, dead or alive.* As the Prince had implied, a
fortune for an individual, wealth for a clan. Was Lord George
Murray planning to earn it, or did the whole mistrust of him,
planted in the Prince's breast, as Elcho now knew, by Murray
of Broughton, arise from Murray's fear of a more powerful
influence, a rival in Charles's councils and confidence? Well,
time would tell.

"Hark!" The Prince's face lit up. "Voices! I hear shouting. Ah! the pipes. Can it mean——?"

It meant victory, bloodless and complete. Edinburgh was
Charles Edward's. Lochiel and his Camerons had marched in
at the Netherbow Port on the heels of the coach conveying
the disappointed deputies, gripped the sentry, and proclaimed
the city to be the Prince's. The little room at the mill was a
babel of men's voices, talking, exclaiming, congratulating.
The Prince, flushed, eager, half-awed, must enter the capital
of Scotland, and the Duke of Perth and his new aide-de-
camp, he vowed, should ride beside him.

Edinburgh, inwardly a hive of dividing loyalties, was outwardly Jacobite and enthusiastic. As he entered, the crowds
cheered and flocked about the Prince, eager to touch his boot
or his horse-furniture, but few threw in their lot with him as
the days went by. Elcho found ample occupation. The following morning the Prince dispatched him to the magistrates of
Edinburgh to demand, under pain of military execution if the
order were not complied with, tents, shoes, targes and canteens.
These were immediately produced, but the requisition did not
increase the young conqueror's popularity. Some three hundred young men were enlisted as life-guards and my Lord
Elcho amused himself by drilling them. As a further mark of
Charles's favour he formed one of the Prince's council. The
daily meetings of these were outwardly smooth and successful,

D

yet there were quarrels, grievances, covert insults offered and received, whilst a day seldom passed without a clash of wills between his Royal Highness and Lord George Murray.

The ancient palace of his ancestors saw nightly revel and entertainment, though the Prince himself declined to take part in any dancing. He preferred to sup and sleep in the camp at Duddingston where his hardy Highlanders, despite the lateness of the season, were occupying tents. Autumn lingers long in Scotland. The courtyard sounded full of the drift and rustle of fallen leaves, and a little frosty wind lifted the ladies' curls as they alighted from their sedan-chairs. The dark shoulder of Arthur's Seat showed its uneven outline against a deep blue sky, and faint lights pricked up in the long slant of the Canongate. The sentries round the door were gaunt Highlanders, reinforced by men picked from some great clan night after night to act as the Prince's bodyguard. The swing of bright tartans was everywhere, the gleam of sword and dirk, the flash of shining eyes. Every woman present was in love with the Prince—that went without saying, reflected my Lord Elcho, bored and contemptuous—but Charles himself, unaccustomed to the fair sex, was cool, shy, almost embarrassed. There was no formality and a vast absence of ceremony. Anybody who wanted to stare at the Prince might walk in, as the Whig faction did, whilst it was no uncommon thing for a staunch Jacobite lady to bring as many as seven daughters to make their obeisance to the Young Chevalier. Candles glowed in the dark gallery, with its silent audience of painted kings, as the hangings at one end parted slowly to frame the slight, stately figure of their descendant. "His Royal Highness the Prince Regent!" Then, like the rustle of the wind over the tops of a field of oats, the ladies' voluminous silks would whisper along the floor as they curtsied to their King's son, and a hundred hands went to a hundred sword-hilts to draw blade in his defence.

A brief, glittering time, but many doubted, even those risking neck and estates in the Royal Adventurer's mad gamble. The Prince himself, for all his high hopes, must, Elcho realized, have known many moments when his ardent spirit quailed before the task he had set himself, and the shadowy crown receded from his eager grasp. Edinburgh's heart was never won. She cheered him, but comparatively few were for the White Rose, and the grim castle remained Whig and undefeated all those six weeks. Even Charles's magnanimity after Gladsmuir, his personal grace and distinction, his clemency

and charm won him a scant number of adherents out of the
town.

England, and ignominious retreat, the fleeting gleam of success which the victory of Falkirk promised, and the grey days
and weeks as the Prince made his last stand. Elcho shrugged
his shoulders. This biting northern cold after the sunshine
of Italy, the caressing warmth of Paris, this creeping realization
of failure, disaster, encroaching perils were bitter bread
indeed. How mad he had been to espouse a Cause which rested
on a nebulous hope of foreign support and an expiring loyalty
to an exiled and unsuccessful House!

The morning had been grey and damp, with anxious vigils
spent awaiting those chiefs and their men still at a distance.
Expresses were sent to hasten the clans engaged in the siege of
Fort William. Lochiel had arrived the previous day and
Keppoch late in the evening. Cluny MacPherson was reported
to be hurrying from Badenoch, but there were many absentees
and deserters, and the want of provisions was deplorably
serious.

The Prince had reviewed his army, and Elcho listened,
smiling a little scornful smile, to the arguments about the
choice of a battle-ground. Of course Lord George Murray
was right. To fight on that bare plain spelt madness, but the
Prince refused to see it. The Irish, as they invariably did,
deferred to his opinion and took his side. Small wonder if
Lord George had thought that that desperate plan of the night-
march offered more hope of success than meeting Cumberland
on the moor. What was passing in the camp at Nairn? Elcho
and his scouts were dispatched to spy out the land.

The landscape was dim and colourless. Under motionless
clouds everything lay remote, indifferent. Faint smoke rose
from a hole in the thatch of a mean cottage. The Nairn reflected the grey face of the low, sunless sky. The air was close,
yet carried no warmth. The little party rode with caution, but
as they neared the outskirts of the Hanoverian camp they met
with no opposition. An uncanny silence reigned. April the
fifteenth was the Duke of Cumberland's twenty-fifth birthday.
When the night-march came to be planned a hope that the red-
coats might be drunk after celebrating the event by loyal
toasts was in all minds, yet surely at such an early hour they
could not have succumbed to their potations? Elcho stared
enviously towards the evidences of abundant war equipment,
the plenty obviously stored, the tents and grazing horses and
waiting cannon. How different from the semi-starvation at

Culloden, the depleted ranks, the meagre, ineffective artillery, the pitiful chance of withstanding such a foe as this! He rode back, musing. At least the enemy was not massing for immediate attack. The Jacobites had the rest of the day to search for food and plan some sort of stand. He had made his report and sat with the others as Charles, summoning his first informal council since Crieff, implored all present to offer their advice. The result had been this mad night-march, ending in failure and anti-climax. Mechanically Elcho reined in and turned his horse to ride back the sodden miles to Culloden House.

CHAPTER V

IAIN MACDONALD, OF KEPPOCH'S CLAN, CURSED THE COLD. HE had known bitter nights, out on the hills with a crude lantern, searching for a strayed sheep, but in the name of the Good Being this was much worse. They said that Tearlach came from a country where the sun always shone, yet he seemed to take no harm from rain or wind or sleet. Oh! he was very brave, this Prince, and one day when Iain had been sent with a message to the chief, Keppoch chanced to be talking to Tearlach, and Tearlach had smiled at Iain. He had a wonderful smile. When you saw it you were reminded of the sun on heather, or gleaming on a blue loch, and you felt that you would put your hands under his feet, or let him do with you what he would. That was at times, of course, when you thought of that smile. At others, you remembered the little croft, with its white-harled walls, and the sheep crying in spring-time, and a man turning up the good earth at the back-end, or sowing in April. Iain heaved a great sigh. The place would be a fair ruin when he returned to it—if he ever did.

Why was he here, plodding through sticky mud, others of the clan shuffling and muttering beside him? They had been promised a battle earlier in the day, but instead were standing on a flat piece of ground for hours whilst the great ones—the Prince, Lord George Murray, Clanranald, Lochgarry, Lochiel, and the tail of Irish Tearlach always had beside him—talked and talked. It was the English tongue, so Iain understood nothing of what they said, but in the end he and the others were dismissed, told there was to be no fighting for the present, and they must eat and rest. How could a man sleep without food inside him? Iain did not understand the way it had happened, but they said there was meal in plenty at Inverness, yet none at Culloden. He felt very hungry. Och! he could be doing with bannocks of his wife Mairi's baking, and ewes'-milk cheese, and a platter of brose. At home, when he came in from the fields, or the market, or the kirk, she had always ample to set before him, and a man could eat in peace and go back refreshed to his work. Why had the Chief sent to him, telling him that Tearlach was come to Scotland, and all loyal men of the clan must gather and fight for him? Iain felt sorely puzzled. If you did not go, what would happen? Bad things, Mairi whispered, shaking her head. They would make you go, fetch you, and the roof would be burned and the kye taken and the children starve. He had thought this mere woman's fears—women were foolish creatures, even the ones like Mairi—but he saw for himself when Hamish MacDonald, his cousin, refused to come out, that all this and worse befell him. Iain had had to go, with the harvest not yet in-gathered, and the peat to stack for the coming winter, and the deal with Duncan MacCoul over the red stirk not completed. Mairi had the three bairns at her skirts, and another to come at Hogmanay, and she could not work the croft single-handed. Her brother Angus was soft, and how were you to trust him to finish any job, even milking the cow or driving her in at nights, or thatching the roof where the storms had damaged it?

There would be plenty to tell Mairi when he came back. He had seen Edinburgh, so much bigger than Inverness, a wonder town, and he had killed a big English soldier, and he and others of the clan had marched over the Border to a country of small fields and hedges in place of stone dykes, and people with hard eyes and bitter mouths. They were frightened of the Highlanders and thought they ate children, so mothers hid their little ones or pretended they had none when the great names of Scotland came that way. England was puny and cold and the rain fell day after day. It was not the wild storms Iain knew, with the sun breaking forth in an hour's time, and everything glistening and refreshed, but a dour drizzle that soaked a man's plaid, and the sky seemed always overcast and grey. He did not know where the army was going. His friend Donald of Clanranald's clan had the English and said there was a town called London, bigger even than Edinburgh, where Tearlach would fight a great battle, a battle to be sung of in the clan-songs ever afterwards, and then his men would march in and he would be king. Eh, man! why could not Tearlach have stayed content with Scotland, far bonnier than England, and satisfied after beating two English armies?

They went as far as a town whose name Iain could not mind, and all the talk was of fighting. Swords were being sharpened and dirks polished and targes made ready, but Keppoch called his children together and told them that instead of the battle they were going back to Scotland. At first Iain did not mind. He might be able to go home and see Mairi and the bairns again. It was too late for the ploughing, but he could do plenty, and when the new wean came Mairi would help him, and in the dark evenings they would sit by their peat fire and he tell her tales of all he had seen. The rest were disappointed that there was no fighting, with killing and plenty of plunder afterwards, and they must turn tail, and surely to God Tearlach did not want to do this? Later, they said that his heart was broken because retreat was forced upon him, and he who had marched on foot at the head of the clans all the way, fording rivers, climbing steep, icy inclines, treading muddy roads as though he walked upon heather, could only sit huddled on his horse, and it was whispered that he and Lord George Murray, the *duine firinneach,* would not speak.

The days were dreary. The English knew that they were retreating and scowled after them and grudged them shelter or food. Iain could not remember much of that ill time, but they left the little towns behind at last and crossed a big river and were in Scotland again. Nobody seemed to know what would happen. Tearlach wanted Stirling Castle, but though he tried his utmost and the Highlanders defeated the English a second time at a place called Falkirk, he had to take his army with him to the Highlands. The winter was very long. Whiles Iain wished that he had slipped away as so many others of the clans had done, and gone back to his croft. No one would know that he was there. It might be thought that he had been killed in the fighting.

He felt sick with hunger and his feet were sore. Even to have Tearlach smile at him, he did not think he could kill an English soldier. Why were they marching so slowly? It had been a while past sunset when the word to start went round, and here was dawn, wan and colourless as are the faces of the dead, showing that day was here. How could they surprise a sleeping enemy now? Iain's hand gripped his claymore. The foe would be awake and ready.

What was that word which came hissing down the drooping

ranks? Return? Return where? To Culloden House, where they said not Tearlach himself could find a morsel of food? The Chief knew best. Keppoch had told his children that they must abandon the attack and go back. Iain's feet floundered along the boggy ground. What did Tearlach matter, or Keppoch, or the English foe? A man must have his meat. When they reached Drummossie, Iain would slip off, make the best speed he could to Inverness, where was meal and perhaps drink, and be with the MacDonalds again before the fighting began. Tearlach would surely not be angered if he knew how empty and weak Iain felt. He must eat and then sleep.

A bird piped thinly near at hand. There was another sound, too, dull, muffled by distance, but Iain knew it. The English drums were beating and the red-coated ones alert.

CHAPTER VI

CULLODEN HOUSE MADE A SQUARE, BALD, FEATURELESS BLOCK in the wan dawning. Lord George Murray strode in with compressed lips and deepening scowl. The failure and abandonment of his cherished plan hurt deeply. His trained eye and experienced mind had told him that it was sheer madness to await Cumberland's advance, notably on the ground favoured by the Prince and his sycophants, and risk a battle. The Highland army must strike first. He had thought out every detail, and for once the Prince and he had been in accord. Everything was divulged to Charles under pledge of the strictest secrecy. The army was to march in a body the ten miles to Kilravock and there divide. Lord George himself and the van would cross the Nairn, march down by the south side of the river, recross near the Hanoverian camp, and attack it from the south. The other column was to march along the north side of the Nairn and, simultaneously with Lord George's, attack from the west. Ker of Graden, that fine staff officer, was dispatched to tell the different commanders to order the men to attack first with their swords. There was great hope that the Duke of Cumberland's soldiers would have been celebrating his Royal Highness's birthday too well and be in no condition to defend themselves. All ought to have fallen out as planned, but instead the delay in marching had killed

the scheme, and the men had undergone unnecessary fatigue
to no purpose.

He trod the hall restlessly. The house felt chill, unfriendly,
yet it represented a last refuge. Would Cumberland strike that
day? If only the Prince's forces could be adequately fed, snatch
some hours' rest, and retire to the uneven, boggy ground on
the far side of the Nairn, at least a battle might not end in
utter defeat and rout. Whose fault was it that the commissariat
arrangements had turned out so hopelessly mismanaged? Lord
George's scowl increased. He had no liking for Mr. Murray
of Broughton, but at least the former secretary proved capable
and efficient. That conceited little lawyer-body, Hay of
Restalrig, originally the Prince's treasurer, and always at his
Royal Highness's elbow, and Colonel O'Sullivan, were indifferent substitutes. Hay was incompetent, far too inclined to
imagine himself indispensable to the Prince as confidential
adviser, whilst scandalously neglectful of his duties of providing for the army's needs, and O'Sullivan—— A bonny
quartermaster-general he was! His laziness was typically Irish.
During the retreat from Derby, when every moment was of
priceless value, he preferred to sit gossiping over a glass of
mountain malaga instead of writing out orders for the next
day's march. He expected others to do his work and then laid
the blame on their shoulders if matters went wrong. Lord
George reflected angrily that he could not be in every place at
the same time. Throughout the entire campaign he had spared
neither strength nor pains to fulfil any duty, but all along he
had been hampered, frustrated, kept back by the malice or
stupidity of those associated with him, and the Prince, head-
strong, unreasonable, prejudiced, did little to smooth his
lieutenant-general's path.

Lord George leaned against a window and stared out. Instead of the leafless park and sodden turf he saw many scenes
from his chequered past. His mind went back thirty years. He
was a young man, hot-headed, much under the influence of
his brother William, and another brother, Charles. Poor
Charles! Life had treated him harshly, and his rash venture
for the Stuarts had ended in irrevocable parental displeasure
and early death. All three had been "out" in the 'Fifteen, and
even now Lord George's thoughts recoiled from the sour
memories of that dismal time. Mar was a weakling, a fool;
Sheriffmuir a fine bungle. The reek of smouldering thatch, the
crying of hungry children thrust out into the snow, their
homes burned over their heads, had never ceased to haunt

him. His own peril and escapes were small matters compared with these——

He was very much a younger son, an undistinguished unit in a large family, and a soldier's career offered the best chance of security and advancement. At eighteen he and his twenty-one-year-old brother Charles were dispatched to Flanders with the hope of their obtaining commissions in the army serving under Marlborough. Rough travelling, strange surroundings and speech, petty debts, harsh treatment from his seniors and superiors—George Murray had known them all. Ill-health was his portion and constantly a nagging want of money. He was an ensign in the first Royals when the Peace of Utrecht brought him with his regiment to England. Four years later, on his way to rejoin the Royals, stationed in Dublin, he had chosen the path which had led him ultimately to where he stood now.

Half-impatiently he recollected his brother, Duke William, as the Jacobites styled him, a prematurely aged man, crippled with gout. Thirty years earlier Tullibardine had been a gallant figure, afire with enthusiasm for the exiled House, slipping away from the parental roof and authority to join the Earl of Mar. Lord George groaned as he realized the dreary likeness between both ill-starred attempts to restore the Stuart dynasty. Mar had promised French aid, a definite rising amongst the English Jacobites, and a visit in person from the Chevalier. Charles Edward had likewise intimated that his landing would be followed by that of a French army, and the conjunction of the Jacobites in England. In neither instance had these events happened. Was the ending now to be the same as it was thirty years since? Would the Prince sail furtively from the shores of Scotland as his father had done, and the chief men who had followed him meet with exile, arraignment, imprisonment, or death?

Lord George supposed grimly that he might consider himself fortunate. After the collapse of the first rising he and Tullibardine lurked for weeks in the Outer Hebrides. Rain, meals of coarse, roughly cooked fish, a suspicious peasantry, the constant watch for a foe or a friendly ship—these made up his memories of the time. In the end he had reached Roscoff in sunny Brittany. Dreary years of existing as best he might followed. Poverty, sickness, heart-hunger for his native land had been his portion. Not until 1719 was another blow struck for the Stuarts, ending, as its predecessor had done, in ruin. Were all risings alike? he mused bitterly. Internal strife and dissensions, secret feuds and clan-jealousies, the envy of one individual for another—all drove a cause to wreck.

He had gained the Continent a second time and concluded sourly that he had learned wisdom. His father, the powerful Duke of Atholl, had the Elector's ear. Mindful of an eldest son fallen at Malplaquet, a younger one dead, unforgiven, after barely escaping the scaffold as a rebel, and his heir a hopeless attainted exile, the stern parent used his influence and secured a pardon for Lord George. He did not resist. The fruits of disobedience and rebellion had been bitter on his lips. It was good to come home to the land which had bred him, to hear the Scots tongue again not merely from those who dragged out their soured, poverty-stricken existences in some little town abroad, to play the farmer, the country gentleman, the one out of all the family to whom the rest turned for advice. The Duke died, and his second son succeeded him. He himself had married, and he was still in love with his Amelia. His face clouded. This business was hard on women. Never had he thought to be more than the laird of Tullibardine, a keen sportsman, watching his children grow up, on the best of terms with his Whig brother, his kinsmen, his neighbours, but the last throw had been made for the falling Cause, and all his old loyalty drove him to serve his King afresh.

From the first his hopes of the success of the Rising had been very faint. He knew the temper of the country and that the time was not yet ripe. France was a broken reed. She would use the Prince to further her own ends and plague England, but Louis XV and his ministers were gracefully indifferent as to whether Guelph or Stuart occupied the throne of Great Britain. Save for the name, the symbol, did it matter? The Stuarts were alien in creed and outlook. If he had succeeded, what make of king would have emerged in Prince Charles?

Lord George Murray shrugged his shoulders. He knew his young leader. Rash, impetuous, brave, but obstinate, stubborn, apt to lend his ear too readily to flatterers and visionaries, a bad judge of men, he had wrecked his own project as much as outward circumstances had contributed to its fall. This grim night's business was only the prelude to the last act.

The man whom the Prince had never trusted thought sombrely of those days when news of Charles's landing had been on every lip. His brother James grew fearful directly he heard that the exile whom he had dispossessed of lands and honours was come to Scotland with the Prince. Duke James took for granted that Lord George would be as much for the Government as himself, and at first Lord George, reasoning coldly, decided to play no part in this third venture for the Stuarts. What had changed his views? What madness had seized him, causing him to fling to the winds his obligations to the reigning House, to risk his wife's health and happiness, his children's futures, for what he considered a principle, a matter of conscience, an affair touching his honour and loyalty? He had staked his very life, alienated his nearest of kin and innumerable friends, jeopardized his remaining years, and to what purpose? He had not even the trust and esteem of the one for whom so much had been sacrificed. From the first the Prince, although at once offering him a post of the highest distinction and responsibility in his army, had been mistrustful of him, had hearkened to tales and insinuations carried to him by the wily and inferior, men such as Murray of Broughton, and seen in his every act a discreditable motive, a cloak for treachery. Lesser things divided them. Charles's impetuosity ill-matched Lord George's blunt outspokenness. He could not bring himself to flatter, to agree with some chimerical scheme proposed by the Prince, and the latter, seeing himself thwarted, sulked and slighted his lieutenant-general almost openly. He will never forgive me for to-night, Lord George decided grimly.

The leaders were straggling in now, all bemused, weary, bewildered. He ought, Lord George realized, to summon the heads of the principal clans and decide upon some plan of action. If they must fight, there should be a rendezvous in case of defeat and withdrawal. He saw how exhaustion and hunger were causing most of the marchers to drop down on chair or floor to snatch a brief repose. The men were in the same case as their officers, seeking sleep in the parks of Culloden or the open country outside. Others, stronger or more adventurous, were heading towards Inverness to find food.

It was morning, but there was no warmth anywhere, nor any life in the colourless atmosphere, the dour landscape.

The Prince was coming. Lord George heard horse-hoofs and braced himself for the inevitable encounter. The Irish and Hay of Restalrig would have been with him, lamenting the retreat, the abandoning of the concerted attack, and laying the blame, as they always did, on Lord George Murray's shoulders. Was there any possibility that Charles would consent to avoid a battle by retiring to the far side of the Nairn?

He must see that to let his army stand to be mown down on
that bald plateau was madness. But when had he ever seen
reason if it conflicted with his own wishes?

The horse halted before the door. Charles slid from the
saddle, disdaining aid, and stood a moment gazing half-
vacantly about him. The shocked thought flooded into Lord
George's mind: *How he has aged!* The Prince looked
pinched, his face drawn and hollow of cheek, dark shadows
under the brown eyes, the mouth compressed and embittered.
When Lord George addressed him he answered like one in a
dream.

"*Hé!* you are here before me, my lord?"

"Yes, sir."

"I cannot understand it." He dragged a hand across his
brow, displacing the Highland bonnet. "We could have
attacked."

"Sir, we could not. The delay in marching was so great
that dawn had come. A surprise attack was impossible."

The Prince stood biting his lip. "What does your lordship
propose instead?"

"The men must have some food, sir, and a certain time to
rest. I will send to Inverness for meal——"

"Good! Good! Tell the inhabitants to send provisions
to my army. Otherwise I will burn the town!"

Lord George's smile was wry. "There is no need for such
extreme measures, sir. We have some cattle we can kill."

"As you please, my lord."

"But your Royal Highness?" Involuntarily Lord George's
tone softened as he contemplated the haggard young face.
"You should rest also, sir, and take at least a cup of chocolate."

The Prince shuddered violently. "Eat! I can neither eat
nor rest while my poor people are starving."

He stared around him, at the bleak landscape, the huddled
forms of men asleep on the ground, the grim-visaged group
of his hungry officers, and swayed a little against the motionless horse beside him. Sir Thomas Sheridan came forward,
limping with fatigue, took his arm, and guided him into the
hall.

CHAPTER VII

A LIGHT BURNED BEHIND THE UPPER WINDOW OF A HOUSE beside a lake, half-way between Inverness and Fort Augustus. The weak yellow flame vied with the sickly dawn beginning to break and make plainer every object in the small bed-chamber where Murray of Broughton lay. He was a sick man, depressed and fearful. The Cause was sinking. He fretted pettishly at his inability to serve it further. Hay was a fool; O'Sullivan little better. They boasted of their intimacy with the Prince and neglected their duties. Murray knew that the meal accumulated in Inverness was sorely needed at Culloden. A half-starved army could not fight. And after further withdrawal—if indeed the Prince could be brought to consent to such a thing—what?

He moved restlessly. The bed was comfortless to his weakened body and everywhere his mind travelled he saw nothing but disaster. His own fate weighed heavily upon him. Enfeebled by illness, how could he make his escape from a country honeycombed with spies and informers? His thoughts stole to his home, the green peace of Broughton, the river where he had fished, the little town by the Tweed. As so many others were doing this night, he cursed the folly, the weakness, the mistaken optimism which had led him into the mad ploy. It could never have succeeded. He saw that now. All along he ought to have seen this.

For years the Cause had been the background of his life. Outwardly he was the douce lawyer, the country laird, the husband of the beautiful toast, Mrs. Murray of Broughton, but secretly he travelled on Jacobite business and his enthusiasm grew. At Rome he had first seen Prince Charles and fallen under the spell of his outward charm and graces. There were many ways in which he could serve. At home adherents must be sought, and he remembered tavern meetings, private gatherings at Edinburgh, when he had striven to stir the slow flame of loyalty into life and to extort promises of support for a rising. They were cold and cautious, these men with whom he dealt. Lochiel remembered all that the earlier rising had cost his father. The Earl of Traquair proved sly, evasive. Young Glengarry, son of a powerful Highland chief, could bring little save his sword, and Lord Lovat—— Murray's small hands, less plump than they had been, clenched angrily on the bed-coverings. Traitor, turncoat, liar, he had safeguarded himself, his estate, his neck throughout. The Frasers had joined the Prince at Bannockburn, but only a mere handful, led by the Master of Lovat, a sulky-lipped boy of nineteen, about whom were varied tales. His father cried him stiff-necked, obstinate, undutiful, flying in his parent's face like a wild-cat, and insisting on bringing out the clan, but this hardly tallied with accounts of secret drilling and arming at Castle Downie, the purchase of tents and warlike equipment, the toasting of the Young Chevalier. Murray grinned weakly. Simon Fraser, Lord Lovat, was no fool.

After Rome—Paris. Again he travelled there in secret and found the Prince installed at the house of Aeneas MacDonald, Kinlochmoidart's brother. The failure of the projected invasion of England spelled ruin to the Stuart hopes, but Charles refused to admit that it was anything more than a temporary set-back. His eyes were on the Highlands. Murray recalled him, young, ardent, enthusiastic, eager to use his sword, his life in any way which should lead to a restoration, but blind to every practical difficulty. The elder man saw how his position, almost penniless, awaiting with impatience any recognition of his claims or person from the King of France, irked the proud spirit. Had he himself been blunt enough, candid enough? Did Charles assume from his (Murray's) talk that if he came to Scotland the Highlands would rise in sufficient strength? Others were only too ready, now that failure, dire and drastic, loomed at hand, to blame the secretary's ill-timed enthusiasm and encouragement. Was he at fault if he, only twenty-nine, had caught something of Charles's fire, ceased to hold him back, and when the landing was accomplishel joined him speedily?

Murray grinned uneasily. He had certainly done his best to cook Balhaldie's goose. Well, it was only right that the Prince should have his eyes opened as to how his agents served him. Balhaldie, supposed to be buying arms for the Cause, gambled in the Sun tavern at Rotterdam, and letters destined for the Prince never reached his hands. Nevertheless, Charles was certain and sanguine, speaking fast and eagerly, declaring that he would be able to procure a body of troops before the winter.

At first Murray hesitated and temporized. He was loath to offer advice upon an affair of such consequence, but certainly the steps to be taken depended very much upon circumstances. Charles shook his fair head gaily. As all events, he averred, he was determined to come the following summer to Scotland, though with a single footman. Murray answered, secretly admiring his own tact, that his Royal Highness could not come to Scotland sooner than would be agreeable to his friends there, but he hoped it would not be without a body of troops. Charles merely repeated what he had said before, speaking with still greater energy. Murray replied that there was danger in coming unless he was sure of assistance. The Prince laughed. Murray could hear the gay sound now. He did not doubt of assistance, but he would come in all events.

A low red sun gilded the stones of the courtyard where the two paced. A pigeon fluttered at their feet, a flash of wings and small rosy feet. Charles said quickly: "How many, *mon ami*, do you think might join me?"

"At the most, sir, I think there would not be above four or five thousand, even if all those whom your Royal Highness looks upon as most attached to your family should join you."

"Four or five thousand?"

"The design is noble, sir, and only becoming a Prince of the greatest spirit, but I think it my duty to show you that in that case you cannot positively depend upon more than four thousand Highlanders, *if so many*."

"But my friends in Scotland, Murray? I have letters, promises——"

"The Duke of Perth, Lochiel, Keppoch, Clanranald, the Stewarts, the MacDonalds of Glengarry, with Cluny and Struan Robertson's people are all your Royal Highness can rely upon with any certainty, sir, from the West Highlands, in case of such an attempt, and even they would be sorry to think you should risk yourself without foreign assistance."

"I will try every method to procure troops, but should that fail, I shall, nevertheless, pay Scotland a visit."

Murray remained silent. Charles went on rapidly: "And the English?"

"Sir, you best know the nature of their engagements and whether they would appear if your Royal Highness came with the Scots alone amongst them."

The brown eyes, the finest he ever saw, Murray averred afterward, flashed. "Provided that I procure such a body of troops as has been offered the preceding spring, few precautions would be necessary. I hope, if they were once landed, all the King's friends would join."

Murray merely bowed and listened.

"I do not doubt of a general rising in Scotland," Charles pursued. He spoke eagerly, enthusiastically. "If Lord Marischal lands with five thousand men. And the English have given me the strongest assurances, nor do I doubt from the offers they have made that they will be less forward than the Scots."

"I trust so, sir."

"I am unalterably fixed in my resolution to make this attempt." The Prince's tone was vehement. "I enjoin you, Mr. Murray, to say on your return to Scotland all the obliging things you are capable of to my friends there, and to acquaint them, in case I do not make a descent upon England, that they may depend upon my appearing among them next summer."

Well, the Prince had kept his word, Murray reflected. It had been one long triumph once the royal standard was set up. He recalled fresh accessions to Charles's Cause, bloodless captures of great cities, the entry into Edinburgh, his wife, erect and beautiful, seated on horseback at the Mercat Cross, distributing white cockades to the favoured, and his own increasing importance and prestige. No doubt—his mouth grew sour—many envied him and sought to drag him from his high eminence. He had the Prince's ear and controlled the privy purse. His thoughts went back to those weeks in Edinburgh. 'Faith! the sullen city had been made to pay. Hay, corn, carts, civic dues—all were demanded. Maclachlan of Maclachlan was commissary-general. His emissaries were told every detail that would assist them in their duties. Murray mouthed one such letter, drafted by himself:

Charles, Prince of Wales, etc., Regent of Scotland, England, France, and Ireland, and the Dominions thereto belonging, to George Gordon, Gentleman. These are empowering you to search for all horses, arms, and ammunition that you can find in the custody of, or belonging to, any person or persons disaffected to our interest, and seize the same for our use—for the doing of which this shall be your Warrant. Given at Holyrood House, the Eighteenth of October, 1745, by his Highness's command.

J. Murray.

An auld sang now, but he had had his day. Others were of small importance beside John Murray of Broughton. Lochiel, Keppoch, Clanranald, Lord Pitsligo—he dismissed the Highland chiefs almost contemptuously. The Dukes of Atholl and

Perth were sickly, negligible, of scant account save for the support each could bring. Lord Balmerino, the Earl of Kilmarnock, the Earl of Nithsdale, Viscount Kenmure. Bah! Nithsdale and Kenmure ran away after pledging their swords and being received most graciously by the Prince. The rest were vague figures. It was Lord George Murray whom the secretary, his namesake, had feared and hated from the start. Lord George was a fine soldier, a strong personality, a powerful influence, and Murray dreaded lest the Prince, easily swayed, obstinate, weak, needing the utmost tact in being governed and advised, should favour him and slight the other.

The task was easy,. almost ludicrously so. He grinned slyly. At times the Prince's swift suspicion of those whom he had no cause to distrust rendered him a ready prey to hint or whispers. Murray murmured his doubts of Lord George into Charles's ear, stressing that Lord George, twice serving the Cause, had at length accepted the Elector's pardon and favour, and who could believe in his protestations of loyalty when he joined the Prince at Perth? That fatal interview with Cope was all Murray needed to blacken Lord George in Charles's eyes. With covert malice and satisfaction he watched the rift grow wider and wider. After the smooth-tongued, subservient Irish the Prince found Lord George's blunt candour distasteful in the extreme. Once Lord George had been goaded into throwing up his commission, but the weight of public opinion, the counsel of wiser heads, compelled Charles to humble himself and request Lord George to withdraw his resignation. The Prince had never forgiven the decision at Derby which forced him to retreat. Murray had often blamed Lord George for having been the predominant voice about this, nor did he fail to point it out to the Prince. Dislike, mistrust, suspicion, incompatibility of temperament, all these had been ripe soil, and into them Murray dropped the dragon-seed which had grown to an ugly harvest.

He stirred and moaned. How had it all ended? Private disputes and petty squabbles, gross mismanagement on the part of those responsible for the feeding and support of the army, the grim knowledge that in the approaching battle the Prince must, almost inevitably, be defeated, and after defeat— panic flight, possible capture, certain death. He was a sick man, a doomed man. In futile misery he cursed the Cause which had drawn him into its toils, the fate that had laid him on a bed of sickness when the Prince needed him most, and the dark, featureless future.

E

CHAPTER VIII

IN THE CAMP AT NAIRN ALL SEEMED QUIET. THE FIRES, ROUND which the Hanoverian soldiers had sat or lounged earlier in the evening, drinking the Duke of Cumberland's health in the two gallons of brandy allotted to each regiment from his Royal Highness's private purse, were burning low. A wind sighed past the tents and went on to lose itself across the rolling moorlands of Inverness-shire. For April everything was cold, reluctant, hindered, unspringlike. The men, accustomed to a more genial clime, shuddered and wondered how the Scots had the stomach to fight in this savage country. Well, to-morrow would show them the English temper, and there should be something to atone for the disgrace of Gladsmuir and Falkirk.

William Augustus, Duke of Cumberland, sat in his tent, his mind also on the coming battle. Where Cope and Hawley had failed he must, he should, succeed. Fontenoy needed to be wiped from the public memory by an overwhelming victory. He yawned, then hunched his shoulders as the tent swayed against a sudden assault of wind. What a country! He could not understand these Scots. For the sake of a Prince, a foreigner, practically Italian through his birth and upbringing, a stranger, although a Stuart, half Scotland, from the greatest names in the land to the meanest peasant tilling his croft, was ready to follow him, to fight for him, if needs be to die for him. Cumberland's own men, dogged English, obeyed and admired their commander, but there was shown him little of this personal affection and loyalty which Charles evoked. It was not his early victories. Directly he set foot on Scottish soil the clans flocked to his standard. What was he like? The Duke had never seen his cousin and a faint curiosity pricked him now. If they met face to face on the morrow, what should he see?

His thoughts strayed back to Edinburgh, in certain respects sullen, disaffected, unwelcoming. He had held state at Holyrood, it was true, but a ghost lurked in the shadows, the ghost of the Stuart Prince, still living, who a bare six months before had entered the old palace, Scotland's uncrowned king. Cumberland, clumsy, ungraceful, awkward, more at home in the camp or on the battlefield than in these thick-walled chambers under the shadow of Arthur's Seat, knew that even those who were avowedly Whig criticized him, compared him with the slim grace of Charles Edward, and not to his advantage. He bit his full lip. They needed a lesson, these barbarous Scots, a resounding defeat, preferably the taking of their leader, and then it would be shown how deep their loyalty to him and his Cause went.

The night was passing. He flung back the tent-flap and gazed out. All showed grey, shadowy, but the sky above and behind the tapestry of the bare trees was lightening, and a wan, cold world beginning to appear. The wind blew in great gusts over dead-looking field and bleak moor. The camp was stirring. Drums and bugles called to arms. Afterwards he realized how the sounds must have carried to the weary, dispirited Jacobite troops straggling back through the muddy woods after the abortive night-march. He threw off his mood. Action! That was what he craved. After weeks of planning and preparation, of waiting until the weather in this accursed country permitted an advance, he was resolved to teach these rebel dogs a lesson.

As the years went he might be considered young, yet he had crowded more into his quarter century of life than many. He was only just nineteen when appointed to the command of the Coldstream Guards. Nineteen in age, but in experience much more. His mouth curled cynically. Certainly his domestic and family background had been a curious one. His grandmother, a name to be spoken in scandalized whispers, was dragging out her slow days in remorseless captivity behind the grim walls of the castle of Ahlden. His father was on ill-concealed terms of dislike with William's grandfather, and a royal whim kept the young Duke separated from his three sisters. True, he was his mother's favourite and her influence had been mainly for good in the undesirable court-life, but as he grew older the fashionable side of the age, its pastimes, its diversions, its modes absorbed his leisure. He had tasted all the current follies: women, cock-fighting, bull-baiting, horse-racing. Vauxhall and Ranelagh were devotedly patronized by him, but his military career meant more to him than all else. He saw active service early. Dettingen . . . Fontenoy. The recollection of the latter clouded his brow. Even the victory of Dettingen was soured by it. He had played his part there and won his laurels, and was only twenty-four (just a year ago, the recollection flashed swiftly into his mind) when gazetted captain-general of all the King's forces in Great Britain, with authority over those employed abroad. His salary was the princely one of three thousand, six hundred and fifty pounds. Those beggarly Stuarts sponged on the Pope, the King of France, on anybody fool enough to subsidize them. He would wager that the Young Pretender was at the end of his resources.

Fontenoy! The scene rose before his eyes now. Instead of a grey Scottish dawn, sunless and leafless scenery, he saw fields green with springing corn, and the church, surrounded by its group of red-tiled, whitewashed cottages. The orchards were snowy with fruit blossom, the fields draped in the mists of early morning. In October he returned to England to crush this impudent attempt at a rebellion. Cope, Wade, Hawley— all had failed. He, William Augustus, Duke of Cumberland, should succeed, and succeed this day, the sixteenth of April, 1746.

His army formed for the advance. Under his eye fifteen red-coated battalions, with the Dragoons of Cobham and Lord Mark Kerr, and Kingston's Horse, making in all between eight and nine thousand men, started to march. Through paling light, as they stepped across the low-lying country gradually ascending to the bare plain of Culloden, they could discern the masts and sails of Admiral Byng's squadron anchored in the Moray Firth. The town of Inverness, miles away, was a misty blot. To west and south there towered the vast bastions of great mountains, now veiled in thin rain. The track was damp and marshy, the wind cutting like a knife, but the Hanoverian army, full-fed, confident, paid no heed. They would give the Jacobites cold steel for breakfast and show their Duke what manner of men Billy commanded.

The day was dank with mist and dark with coming sleet.

CHAPTER IX

MR. EVAN BAILLIE OF ABERICHAN INHALED SNUFF AND BE-came extremely thoughtful. There was, of course, a risk, a considerable risk. He must expose his person, possibly become involved in the conflicting elements, but on the other hand, to view from a safe distance a battle between the forces of Prince Charles Edward and those of the Duke of Cumberland was a temptation hard to be resisted. His friend, Mr. Maxwell of Morphy, had ridden out to Aberichan with certain intelligence that the battle was imminent. There was decided

movement about the Hanoverian camp at Nairn, and at Culloden the Prince's forces were said to be assembling.   Mr.
Maxwell did not venture to speak too positively, to affirm
it as an ascertained fact, but he had heard talk, nay, more
than a rumour, that the Jacobites the previous night had
marched to attack the Hanoverians in their stronghold.
Eagerly Mr. Baillie inquired what had resulted.   Mr. Maxwell
shrugged his shoulders.   His information, possibly garbled and
incorrect (these days any number of wild stories were current),
was to the effect that the Pretender had turned tail——   "Nay,
Aberichan, you need not look so angry, man.   It may not be
true."

"I am certain that it is not, sir."

Mr. Maxwell smiled.   He had always strongly suspected his
friend of Jacobite leanings, but this confirmed what his politics
were.   A trifle unwise to display such heat.

"Well, well, we must not believe all we hear."   He spoke
smoothly, soothingly.

"If it is true"—Mr. Baillie's tone was stiff—"I fear it may
impair the Prince's chances of beating his adversary."

"Why so, sir?"

"His army will be fatigued, and I heard further that their
stock of provisions is vastly reduced."

"Tut! tut!"

The two gentlemen eyed one another thoughtfully.

"You have not yet said whether you will fall in with my
proposal," Mr. Maxwell murmured.

"To view the battle from a distance?"

"Precisely."

"Really, sir——   It requires consideration.   I am mighty
busy."

"But it may prove the occasion of a lifetime."   Crafty Mr.
Maxwell baited his hook with extreme care.

"That is certainly true."

"And to see both the protagonists——   I shall certainly go."

"In that case——   I suppose my correspondence could
wait."   Mr. Baillie pushed back his wig.   "Where did you say
the Prince's troops were assembling."

"On Drummossie Muir."

"An unwise choice.   That bare plain!   Who selected it,
sir?"

"I regret that I am not in a position to have the felicity
of informing you.   Who commands after the Pre—the Prince?"

"My Lord George Murray, I believe."

"Then doubtless he is responsible."

"I can scarce credit Lord George with such folly. A soldier, one to whom the Prince's two previous victories are largely due, to expose an army to the fire of their adversaries on a naked moor—— Pooh!" Mr. Baillie nearly upset his snuff-box in the heat of his indignation.

"We need not dispute over such a trifle, sir. Time—nay, to-day, the next few hours—will assuredly decide——"

"The fate of Scotland?"

"I would not go so far." Mr. Maxwell dipped two fingers absent-mindedly in his host's proffered mull. "Shall we say—the fate of Tearlach?"

Mr. Baillie winced and shook his head.

Curiosity, his own private inclination, a shame-faced patriotism drove him to fall in with his friend's suggestion. The two mounted their horses and rode out through the raw morning. It was nearly midday, but mist, dank and chill, shrouded the landscape. The young larch in the plantations was still hindered. Wide, treeless spaces were bleak, colourless, sunless. The great mountains showed no more than their outlines against a pallid sky. The air bit naggingly.

"I doubt we shall have snow," prophesied Mr. Maxwell cheerfully.

"Snow? 'Tis the sixteenth of April, sir."

"I smell it in the air."

"Will that affect the Prince's chances?"

"At Gladsmuir and Falkirk the weather was in his favour. Here, I cannot but think much depends upon the position his army takes up. If they have the wind in their faces and it should snow or sleet——"

Mr. Baillie shook a rueful head. Since learning that the battle was to be fought on the exposed plateau styled Drummossie Muir his hopes for the Prince had waned. Mr. Maxwell, a shrewd and experienced countryman, was weatherwise. Surely snow threatened in that snarling wind which blew towards them, and the few hard particles beginning to drop from those dour clouds overhead were sleet? Aberichan had passed a night of sound sleep in a comfortable bed, and on rising had partaken of an ample and leisurely breakfast, but those unfortunate Highlanders, if his friend's tale were true, must have marched for hours, covering many miles, in the abortive attempt to attack the enemy's camp, and were practically starving. What condition would they be in to face well-fed, well-equipped, rested troops, ay, and trained soldiers, every man of them?

He lived on his estate out by Inverness and the stir and turmoil of the Rising had not affected him personally. He was a widower, with no sons to espouse either side. As though it were the scenes enacted in some drama on the boards he watched, his sympathies secretly with the Prince, the different stages of the struggle. He learned of the landing, the taking of Edinburgh, the defeat of Cope, and the advance into England. So smoothly, so successfully had Charles progressed that Mr. Baillie confidently anticipated hearing next of his entry into London. He had shaken a nation's foundations, set the throne rocking, sent panic into the hearts of stolid citizens, and won half Scotland to his standard. Then had followed weeks of uncertainty, when rumour travelled northward, nay, a pack of rumours. Some said that the headlong advance had been checked at Derby. Others hinted at a discreditable rout. Be that as it might, in the end the wild clans and their leader reappeared in Scotland again. Mr. Baillie kept a finger in several commercial pies and knew that Glasgow was expecting the invaders. Charles had gone there and made the city pay heavily for espousing the Hanoverian side. Afterwards came news of the Government troops meeting a devastating defeat near Falkirk, and Major-General Hawley joined Sir John Cope in the company of discredited commanders. What now? Mr. Baillie and neighbouring lairds asked one another this with growing eagerness, slightly tinctured by apprehension. Was it possible that the Pretender would make a stand in the north? He was assuredly coming there. In time he took Inverness, obliging Lord Loudoun to depart in somewhat indignified haste to the Black Isle. He left a garrison at Inverness, but this very soon surrendered to the Prince. Even my Lord President Forbes was forced to sail to Skye, accompanied by Lord Loudoun and MacLeod of MacLeod. There were tales about MacLeod and whispers and shrugged shoulders. It was said of him that in the event of a rising he had promised to support the Prince and had afterwards gone back on his word. Well, others had done the same. Mr. Baillie was very well with Forbes of Culloden and knew that he nourished the deepest suspicions of my Lord Lovat——

He himself had had the felicity of seeing the Prince more than once. Charles was in Inverness itself, or staying in the neighbourhood at Castlehill or Culloden. Once, returning home in a dim spring dusk, the laird of Aberichan met a party of horsemen riding towards the town. The foremost was tall and fair-haired, with a pride and carriage which distinguished him from his companions. Mr. Baillie abandoned the convictions of a lifetime on meeting those large brown eyes as the Prince raised his bonnet and smiled. Well, it was something to have seen the disturber of Scotland in the flesh, to describe him to later generations, to wish him well secretly, but after to-day what must his fate?

The wind was bitter and the sleet stung. How would this spiteful cold feel to one nurtured in kings' palaces, but now hungry, harassed, and partially defeated? Mr. Baillie shook a wary head. He was sorry, too, for the chiefs—Lochiel, who had striven to civilize his clan and improve his people's lot, the heads of the three MacDonald clans, men like the Duke of Perth, or Lord Pitsligo, genuinely and unselfishly devoted to the Cause. If the Duke of Cumberland were victorious—and 'faith! it seemed mighty likely—ruin, desperate, overwhelming, and complete awaited all these. A rebellion was a cursed business. It took the tacksman from his little farm, the bonnet-laird from his croft, the eldest son from his studies, and the ragged Highlander from his poaching and his starveling fields. It led—it could lead—to nothing but misery, want, despair, and wreck. They knew nothing, the common men, for whom or what they fought. Blindly they followed the beckoning of a chief's finger, or their homes were destroyed. It was clan-rule, clan-custom. And he, that smiling, yellow-headed young man, erect on his bay horse, what were his thoughts, his feelings, this dour April morning? Did he see defeat, disaster, the crushing of high hopes and lawful ambition, or was he still preparing to make a stand, to rely on his past victories, to nurse an incurable optimism, an unconquered hope?

"We are not the only spectators, I perceive," Mr. Maxwell remarked.

Certain country folk and a parcel of curiosity-mongers from Inverness itself were taking the same road as the two horsemen. No doubt word of an impending battle was abroad. The prospect meant a little stir and colour in drab lives. Some were for the Prince; others on the side of law and order; the majority bewildered, neutral. A gloating curiosity showed in most faces. The rest looked scared or sluggishly indifferent. Mr. Baillie was excessively annoyed to observe his own blacksmith among the gaping rabble. He had no business to neglect his work in this fashion merely to watch from a safe distance the horrid spectacle of men slaughtering one another.

"Curiosity is a most unpleasant failing." He spoke sententiously.

"But surely a pardonable one? They do not see a prince every day—two princes." Mr. Maxwell laughed.

The Nairn lay cold and lifeless under the steel-grey sky. Sleet fell slowly, reluctantly, in small, stinging particles. As the two gentlemen rode nearer they saw, some way off, men drawn up in line, the majority wearing weather-stained tartans. There seemed to be about five thousand, at a rough estimate, but Mr. Baillie's searching eye could not discern more than sixteen guns. What force had the enemy? Probably he could put twice as many soldiers in the field, not to speak of superior artillery. What folly, what crazy obstinacy had led the Prince to choose such a battle-ground, or, for the matter of that, to fight at all?

CHAPTER X

IT WAS FULL DAWN WHEN RANALD CAMERON AWOKE. AS HE struggled back to uneasy consciousness he wondered stupidly where he was and how he came to be in such a situation. His clothes were soaked with dew and damp. He felt stiff, chilled to the bone, stupid from hunger and fatigue. Only half aroused he sat up on one elbow, the other hand plucking idly at a little green root growing beside him, whilst his mind strove painfully to piece together the events which had led to his finding himself here. The place was a wood, with a sickly light filtering through the trees, and a cold wind breathing in his face. His feet and legs felt like lead, save that lead has no sensation, and all his limbs ached and tingled. As in some other life he recalled confusedly an unending march. Why? Whither? Where had he come from, and for what place was he bound? Nairn—Nairn. The name drummed in his brain like the tolling of a bell. Ha! was it not at Nairn that the forces of the Duke of Cumberland were encamped? Ay, and the Prince's army had orders to march by night and attack them. Night! Instead of her kindly curtain the greyness of a wan dawn was seeping everywhere. He stared about him, his fingers unconsciously grasping the tiny root which he had dragged from its shelter in the soil. How far was he from Culloden? What had become of the long column out of whose ranks he had staggered for a brief respite? A hot flush of shame dyed his cheek as he realized that the short rest he had sought whilst the men were halted had lengthened to a prolonged sleep from which he had only just awakened.

Where was he? Where was the Highland army? Had the attack been made? Surely, in that event, the noise would have aroused him, or someone had shaken him back to consciousness? Stifling a groan, he crawled stiffly to his feet and stood contemplating his surroundings. A few paces further on there seemed to be a break in the wood. He made his way, stooped and shivering, walking like an old man, towards this, and saw, beyond the gap, the outlines of a small farmhouse. His stomach craved for food. Even if the people dwelling there were not in sympathy with the Prince's Cause, they could hardly refuse him a morsel of food or a draught of milk? He stumbled on, curiously light-headed and bemused. At least, supposing his hunger stayed unsatisfied, he might learn what had happened whilst he slept that ill-starred sleep.

The place seemed a croft of the better sort. In that pale dawn the newly sown fields smelled fresh and springing. The scent of peat-smoke hung in the air and birds were carolling. Dew jewelled the spiders'-webs between the stakes of a rough paling. How remote, how peaceful it all appeared compared with the din of battle, the lust to kill, the glitter of dirk or broadsword, the petty cabals and intrigues of the Prince's camp. Many dawns had he risen early and gone down to the river to fish, looking in at the dairy on his way for a drink of the newly brought in milk and a jesting word with the dairy-lass. Instinctively his steps took him towards the white-harled shed beside the house from whence he could hear the stamp of cattle-hooves and a strain of low singing. He thrust open the door.

Within, all was dusk-dark, save for a shaft of light slanting down from a strip of cobwebbed window. A girl sat beside a cow, her head pressed against its dun flank, her deft fingers busy with the oozing teats. Her song was an old milking ditty which Ranald had heard since his cradle. He set his teeth at the bitter-sweet memories it evoked.

His form loomed in the low doorway. The girl turned, ceased her task, and looked at him. She showed no alarm at his dishevelled appearance, but gave him a greeting in the Gaelic. Her speaking voice was as full and as rich as her singing one.

"What is this place?" he asked her.

"It is called the farm of the Yellow Knowe."

"And—— Where am I? Is this far from Inverness?"

Her brows, moth-faint in a pale face, met. "Inverness? That is a long road away. Nairn lies four miles beyond."

Nairn! Here the Prince's foes were gathered. He winced wretchedly.

"What do ye seek?" she queried.

"I—do not know." He dragged a hand across his brow. "Have you seen aught of a body of men passing?"

She shook her head.

"We are peaceful folk here. They say there will be fighting and the Duke's soldiers are waiting to attack, but I do not understand war."

He leaned against the side of one of the stalls. The place smelled of straw and the pools of peat-water collected along the uneven floor. The little window made a colourless square in the dark roof overhead.

"War is foulness." His voice shook. "It means death and maiming and ruin, and the crushing of the innocent who have done no harm."

She said slowly: "If Prince Tearlach had never come to Scotland, we had stayed at peace."

He could not argue. Had that bright figure, seeking his own, not landed in the Western Isles some eight months earlier, Ranald Cameron and so many like him would have pursued his even existence, knowing nothing of politics or battles, caring only for the life of the soil, the tilling of the good earth, receiving its benefits, wooing Nature as one woos a woman, realizing her to be fickle, variable, ay, even treacherous, yet wholly lovable. Now, he was not even with the others swept into the maelstrom of this mad rising. He felt fugitive, forlorn, bewildered, as much uprooted as the frail plant his hand unconsciously clutched. As he stood he swayed——

"Where are ye from?" the girl whispered.

"Culloden."

"And how did you come here?"

"We marched all night. I left the column and fell asleep. I do not know what has happened. Was there a battle?"

She shook her head again.

"The red-coated ones were drinking their Duke's health. Even here you could listen to the shouting and singing. I was up with a cow which had fallen sick, and there were men halting outside and a great press of voices, but I cannot tell you whose they were."

"The Prince's army. And then?"

"A trampling that seemed to last for hours. It was as though they marched back the way they had come."

A retreat—and without striking a blow! He groaned aloud.

"Are ye sick?"

"No. That is—— I am hungry."

"I will fetch you bannocks and the milk is newly drawn."

His frown deepened. "Why should ye feed me? Are you for the Prince?"

"I know naught of him. All I see is that you are faint for fasting. Sit here." She rose from her stool and thrust the rough seat towards him. "Can you milk?"

He laughed hoarsely. "Why, yes."

"Then finish the dun cow. She does not heed a strange hand."

He lurched towards the stool and collapsed obediently upon it. The smell of the cow's warm, hairy body was soothing, drugging. Mechanically his hands sought the udders and the even swish-swish of the sound as the milk fell into the pail made a little music through the silence. His task was half-completed when the girl came back. She carried some rough oat-cakes, smeared with butter.

"Eat," she ordered briefly. "And here is a vessel for the milk."

She dipped a rough wooden cog into the bowl's foamy contents and held it towards him.

Ranald Cameron forgot his manners, his Highland courtesy, and grabbed at the cog. She smiled, slowly, understandingly, as he gulped down the warm draught and gobbled the oat-cakes. He had risen to his feet to take these from her. She resumed her place on the stool and finished the milking, her face averted from him whilst he ate and drank wolfishly. The simplicity of the gesture brought stinging tears to his eyes——

"How can I thank you?" His voice was rough, shaking.

"It is nothing. You are hungry, and that is plain fare."

"It was manna." Again he laughed feebly.

They looked at one another. Two strangers, neither knowing the other's name, Fate had linked them together for a brief space ere parting them ruthlessly again. He must go back to uncertainty, hazard, danger, possibly death. For her there remained the dull, monotonous round of duties on the croft, an unending struggle with the soil, the chills of winter, easing the needs of dumb beasts, the harsh realities of wind, rain, and mist. He smiled at her. She smiled back.

"I do not know how ye are called."

"Peggie. Hereabouts they say Peggie of the yellow hair."

He saw, suddenly, that in that dim place her hair shone like stooked corn under a noon sun. An impulse came to him to put out his roughened hand and stroke it, but he held back.

"My name is Ranald Cameron. I am of Lochiel's clan," he told her.

Simply she repeated the syllables. "Ranald Cameron of Lochiel's clan. I shall remember," she said.

He moved slowly towards the door. As he opened it he noticed that the light had grown stronger and the day was fully come. What might have chanced ere its ending?

The girl came up and stood peering over his shoulder. The sight both saw held them spellbound.

Below the fields that framed the little croft was open country. Along it, in steady, relentless formation, there marched three columns of infantry, with cavalry at front and rear. The Duke of Cumberland's army was on its way to Drummossie. Ranald Cameron stayed blinking after it. To his tired eyes it seemed endless, unending, and against its might would stand the depleted, half-starved ranks of the Prince's definitely inferior force.

His thoughts raced and swerved. What had happened to the men and officers who had made the night-march? Were they back at Culloden House, seeking rest and food, lulled into temporary security, or had they fled beyond the Nairn to a safer position? There was no answer to these questions, but his brain recognized one thing only. The Prince must be warned of the impending danger. Then he became aware that the girl was speaking, low, urgently.

"You can travel faster than they. Go by the wood until you come to a place where three ways meet. Take the one to your left, and you should reach your Prince before those men can be there."

He muttered brief thanks.

Peggie of the yellow hair passed from his thoughts as he set his stumbling feet in the direction she had indicated. It was still cold and grey, but he judged the time to be about eight o'clock. The rough track seemed endless. He walked, then broke into a run, almost fell on a treacherous patch of slimy mud, recovered his balance and pressed on. A place where three ways meet. In the darkness the night before he had failed to notice this. To his eyes now the landscape all seemed alike, boggy ground, bare trees, here and there a sunken dyke. Oh,

for wings, a horse, any means of locomotion other than his own
sore feet and aching limbs! Ahead, he saw a break in the
wood and lurched towards it. As he came nearer the path
split into three. One of these slanted towards the left. He
followed it and found that it ran down into rough fields, dank
with mist. His sense of direction was confused and blurred,
but it seemed that if he went ahead he must reach Culloden.
Once he halted and looked back. A long blur, moving forward,
told him that the Duke's army was continuing its relentless
march.

He fought against the desire for renewed sleep. He must
not falter or fall. On and on he stumbled, through the dull,
blind morning, which seemed to have no clarity or life. Everything was grey: the dark sky, the cold gleam of the Nairn, the
sodden grass he trod. Sleet was falling, he realized, and a little
later it dissolved in soft rain. It beat against his bent face
and pearled his plaid. A few remembered landmarks thrust
themselves upon his consciousness as he blundered past. There
was the roofless cottage, reputed to be haunted, and further on
a larch plantation. He must be nearing Culloden. Those
were the park walls, and a wild, tattered Highlander suddenly
rose up and in barely intelligible Gaelic demanded his name
and business.

"I must see the Prince," Ranald stammered.

"Why?"

"I bring news."

The man answered that Tearlach was very thrawn at the
failure of the night-march. Was he at the house? Yes, and
Lord George Murray and the chiefs. The sentry let Ranald
pass, and the young man tottered and lurched the last few
yards which seemed more like miles.

Everything inside appeared and felt as lifeless as the
policies. The hall showed men sleeping in haphazard, uncomfortable attitudes. Neither voices nor any movement sounded
from adjacent rooms. Ranald stared about him, seeking for
someone in authority. A length he shook roughly the shoulder
of the nearest sleeper, a young officer wearing the Ogilvy tartan.

"Wake up!"

"Leave me alone," muttered the other. "I must sleep, if
there is no food."

"Wake up!" Ranald repeated the word insistently. "I
bring news. Where is the Prince?"

"I do not know." A frown stressed the answer as the
speaker struggled with a mighty yawn. "His Royal Highness

came in after he had spoken to Lord George Murray at the door."

"Can I see Lord George?"

"Ask another. I have no idea where he has gone."

Ranald muttered an impatient malediction on the drowsy lad from Angus and made his way upstairs.

The house felt unnaturally still. As a rule some of the Irish were about, talking volubly or laughing in the loud, empty-headed, volatile fashion which never failed to exasperate the sober Scots, but now he saw only shut, secretive doors, and heard not so much as a whisper. It was as though a spell had fallen on the place, plunging all beneath the roof into sleep or silence. At length, after waiting irresolutely, he knocked on the nearest door. After a pause Lord George Murray emerged. In the strengthening light he looked old, incredibly fatigued, but still indomitable. His voice came harshly, throatily. "Your business, sir?"

"I have news, my lord."

Lord George waited.

"The enemy is on the march."

"How far off is he?"

"Some miles, my lord."

"And you saw him?"

A red flush of shame dyed the young man's face.

"I was with the Camerons on the night-march and I—I stepped aside while a halt was made. Your lordship will find it hard to pardon me—Lochiel also—but I fell asleep, and—and——"

"I do not blame you. We are all wearied and hungry. Well?"

"When I woke it was dawn. I was alone. I—I found a croft where a woman gave me milk and told me my direction. We saw the Duke of Cumberland's men moving. It looked—it looked a great army."

"This was some distance from here?"

"I should judge it so, my lord."

"Then we have yet time to assemble our ranks. I will inform the Prince. Make your peace with Lochiel, young man, and rejoin your clan. It is well you brought word of this advance, or the enemy might have taken us unawares."

Lord George nodded curtly and withdrew into the room from which he had so lately emerged.

Ranald Cameron stood leaning his shoulder against a wall. Unseeing, his eyes stared down through the window beside him.

It framed a dim vista of the park, and figures, lessened to dwarf's proportions, crossed it like moving dots. Dully he strove to carry out Lord George's directions. He was to seek Lochiel, crave forgiveness for his dereliction of duty, and take his place among the Cameron clan in readiness for the coming battle, but his limbs felt leaden and uncertain, his brain dulled and stupid. What was the use of standing to be mown down by the red-coats? Would the Prince consent to cross the Nairn and take up a position which might at least delay decisive defeat? He lounged listlessly, his ears hearing vaguely a sound of voices in the room behind, voices raised and heated as though in argument or dispute. At length the door crashed open and Lord George emerged, his frown darkening his face until the boldest might have slunk aside, his lips muttering wrathfully. Ranald caught the words "incredible obstinacy," "crazy folly," "ruin for us all," ere Lord George's eye fell upon him. He halted before plunging down the staircase.

"Did I not order you to rejoin your chief, young Cameron?"

Ranald started. "Your pardon, my lord."

"Go at once! The Prince insists on fighting on the moor. We shall need every claymore."

Ranald echoed vaguely: "On the moor?"

"You heard me."

"But—but 'tis madness, my lord."

"Well, go in and plead with his Royal Highness to change his mind. You may have better success than I."

CHAPTER XI

DONALD CAMERON OF LOCHIEL, NICKNAMED THE FAIR-HAIRED one, huddled uneasily in the comfortless chair which his kinsman, Dungallon, had thrust towards him when they reentered Culloden House. He was so weary that all coherent thought seemed to have fused into vagueness, nothingness. He knew, wretchedly, haphazardly, that he ought not to sit there. He should be up, stirring, doing something. Where were his Camerons? They needed food as badly as, God knew, their chief needed it. Hunger ate into a man like rust. What could be done? The night-attack, in addition to failing starkly, had fatigued and discouraged the army. He heard vague whispers of further desertions and tales of men heading for Inverness in quest of provender. His mind went back over the last few months, seeing a series of pictured incidents, but with little that stood out distinctly or clearly. Folly to loll here, recalling the useless past, but he was tired, tired——

The heat of the July day was like a dream remembered against this grey, chill April. He saw the face of his brother Archibald, as he had dispatched him to the Prince to beg Charles to return to France. Charles had refused, haughtily, decisively. Young Scotus was sent to Lochiel with a message, reminding the Cameron chief of his duty. Duty! There had been a bargain struck, but the Prince had failed to fulfil his part. Where was the French aid that he had agreed to bring if the Highlands consented to rise? Lochiel remembered that tavern meeting at Edinburgh many months before; Murray of Broughton, newly returned from Paris, confident, enthusiastic, full of the Prince's courage, enterprise, and charm; Lord Lovat, gross, sly, sneering; young Glengarry; MacLeod of MacLeod; my Lord Traquair, slippery, boastful, a broken reed; and himself, seeing clearly the hazards, but willing to serve his king. He remembered riding through hot, ripe country, the yellow of the corn on every hand, and the long patches of heather purple under the sun. His brother Fassefern, shrewd merchant, had warned him, applauded his resolve to refuse to join the Prince, sought to turn him from his purpose of merely seeing Charles. The little ship tilting in the blue water of Lochnanuagh, the close cabin, with that regal young figure awaiting him, the golden head against the dark boarding. Charles had pleaded passionately with him, taunting him with failure to keep his word, and in the end he had yielded. He left behind him all security, the pleasant life of responsibility and duty which had contented him for many years, and went blindly into an enterprise as mad as it was gallant. Fool? Yes, thrice fool, but what of honour, faith, pledged word and solemn oath and covenant?

He remembered the night at Gray's Mill, the waiting, the tension, and the strategy which had won Edinburgh for Charles without the firing of a pistol or the drawing of a claymore. At least the honour there lay with him and his Camerons. Despite fatigue and lassitude he grinned feebly as he recalled the sentry's foolish, gap-toothed stare when the clan rushed in through the gate on the heels of the returned coach, and the sensation of his own hand gripping the man's shoulder. After that, and still more following Gladsmuir, there had been victory, splendour, state, but how hollow, how unstable, how—in a measure—unreal, those six weeks of triumphal reign in Edinburgh seemed. It was autumn, with a sad wind singing

·round the massive walls of the old palace, and rustling the drift of leaves in the courtyard. He saw men at the council table, and heard voices raised in the exchange of argument. England? There was talk of Wade at Newcastle. Why not rest content with Scotland? In the end the Prince had won his way and his army marched out of Edinburgh, their faces set to go to London. It had been November, a sad, colourless morning, the long fields outside the town empty and rough with stubble, the Forth pallid and motionless, a thin wind keening, the townsfolk dour, expressionless, but their hearts rejoiced. If there were weeping behind shuttered windows the town showed it not.

The Esk. He saw it wide and clear and the great mass of Highlanders fording it steadily. On the far bank they halted and there was a dazzling glitter of bared steel as every man drew sword or claymore and faced Scotland with uplifted weapon. Lochiel's mouth twisted. His own sword slipped, how, none could tell, least of all himself, and the bright blood ran over his hand. The Prince had been concerned and gracious, coming to bind up the trivial wound with his own handkerchief, a lace-edged French toy, but Lochiel saw lengthened faces and heard whispers of the accident being a bad omen. Too true. From the start, despite its initial, elusive success, the Rising was fated, doomed. He saw Derby, a maze of wet, mean streets, and remembered how the royal standard, hoisted carelessly, had overturned and lay broken. A second omen, a second warning, many muttered. Then the confused weeks of retreat and the bitter knowledge of failure stabbed afresh. Glasgow, and the sour faces, and mumbled maledictions, and reluctant disbursing of gear and money for the rebels' needs. The army was angered and reckless. He had had to exert his authority to prevent his Camerons looting and destroying. He saw the Prince, cold and proud, on horseback in his French finery. Charles dressed with greater care and elegance in the rich Whig city than he had done anywhere else, but he won no smiles, no support. Glasgow was glad at his departing——

He dreamed, a confused dream, of the vale at Glenfinnan and his long march at the head of his men to where the Prince waited to raise the royal standard. The sun burned the heather so hotly that it was as though they trod in flame. A curlew was crying overhead. The pipes wailed in the stillness. He recalled that proud young face and the smile that softened it at the Highlanders' shout: *Prionnsa Tearlach Righ nan Ghaidheil!*

Well, he had tasted triumph, but must it not make the bitter cup of defeat now offered to his lips taste more brackish and sour?

A hand was on Lochiel's shoulder, shaking him. He stirred and sat erect. One of his Camerons, young Ranald of Invershalloch, was bending over him, speaking urgently. The enemy was advancing. He had sighted them. The Prince was determined to give battle. The army must be mustered. What were Lochiel's orders?

"Orders?"

"Yes, Lochiel. We wait for you."

Groaning, Lochiel struggled to his feet. The unwelcome tidings that the foe were on the march had begun to spread from lip to lip. Other chiefs were alert, seeking their clansmen, ready to hound those remaining to the site of battle. Ranald saw black looks, lowering faces, and heard muttered disapproval and resentment. He shrugged his shoulders. It was all mad, foredoomed, but there could be no turning the Prince from his purpose.

The morning was still raw, misty, inclining to rain or sleet. The men would have no stomach to fight. Lochiel preceded Ranald out of the door just as the Prince came down the staircase. Ranald saw that he still wore the damp tartans and mud-encrusted boots in which he had marched or ridden all night. The grey light showed him worn, haggard, pallid, but his lips were pressed together obstinately and his eyes, glazed for want of sleep, stared angrily, suspiciously. He spoke to none until the Duke of Perth, a wraith and no man, came forward and addressed him. The high voice, husky, throaty, answered audibly.

"*Comment?* The Marquis D'Eguilles desires to speak with me?"

"He craves the honour of a quarter of an hour's private audience, sir."

"Now? What can he have to say?"

The Duke remained discreetly silent. There was a little smirr of fine rain against the windows.

"It is vastly inconvenient, Perth. I should be seeing that my army is drawn up in order of battle."

"Would you not grant the Marquis this favour, sir? I can engage that he will not delay your Royal Highness's motions."

"*Eh bien——*" Charles bit his lip, moved towards a small room opening off the hall, and nodded briefly. "Request him to join me, but I cannot give him any length of time."

CHAPTER XII

ALEXANDRE DU BOYER, MARQUIS D'EGUILLES, TITULAR FRENCH
Ambassador, sidled into the apartment on the heels of the
Duke of Perth's intimation that his Royal Highness the Prince
Regent had been graciously pleased to grant him an audience.
Hé! but this was a ticklish business. Fervently he wished that
anybody else—milord George Murray, or his brother, or His
Grace of Perth, or one of the Irish, or even that cock-sparrow
Monsieur Hay of Restalrig—had undertaken the task. The
Prince was charming, but unstable, courageous, but obstinate,
and he believed himself invincible because he had not yet been
beaten. Could he not see—*hélas!* could none make him see?
—the irreparable folly of fighting? He was defied by enemies
whom he thoroughly despised, and saw at their head the son
of his father's rival, all of which, coupled with his own pride
and haughtiness, refused to allow him to admit the possibility
of defeat. When the Frenchman entered he was standing by
the window, gazing out at the dreary panorama of park, the set
of his shoulders displaying implacable decision. As Charles
turned the Marquis bowed deeply. The Prince gave him a
hand to kiss.

D'Eguilles smiled wryly. He knew that his position had
never been fully explained to those about the Prince, and many
believed that he brought Charles French promises still unful-
filled. His thoughts went back to that uneasy voyage from
France in the previous autumn, a voyage which after sea-
sickness, alarms, and narrowly escaped perils by shipwreck
or capture ultimately landed him at Montrose on a gusty
October evening. *Mon Dieu!* what a country. The cobbles of
the quay were greasy and slippery, the place stank of fish, a
wind whirled his cloak in all directions, a woman bearing a
great basket full of herrings thrust insolently against him, and
when he remonstrated haughtily let loose a torrent of what he
supposed must be personal abuse in a totally unknown tongue.
He arrived at Holyrood, conscious of little save faces stupid or
scowling, a damp, reeking, unpleasant mist clouding everything, perpetual rain or east wind, and the disagreeable sensation of being in a city held only insecurely by the Stuart Prince.
The palace, after the gaiety and splendour of the French court,
repelled him by its darkness and dourness. Tall, grim-visaged

men, strangely clad and equipped, seemed to be everywhere. The apartments were mean, furtive, comfortless. The sea-coal fires gave out little heat, and his valet complained bitterly of the inadequacy of the arrangements for brewing the Marquis's chocolate. Gaston and Monsieur Richard Morison, his Royal Highness's body-servant, were constantly at loggerheads. He disliked the castle, towering over the narrow, crowded city, with its Hanoverian garrison and its Whig commander. The Scots ladies who came to the Prince's court were plain, homely, with no arts or graces. The Prince himself——

The foreigner had never seen Charles before. King Louis took extreme care to keep the young man at a good distance from his person. The Prince might be useful as a weapon to strike at those accursed English, but it was another thing to set him upon the throne of Great Britain. D'Eguilles received his orders and understood a good deal more which was never put into words. He thought of all this as Charles granted him his first audience, and whilst they chatted in French, recalling mutual acquaintances, and the new ambassador hinted at the French king's purposes, D'Eguilles privately summed the Prince up——

There was another man, unknown to him, as he was unknown to D'Eguilles, who saw Charles only briefly, yet read him shrewdly and thoroughly. During the royal invasion of Blair Castle, Bisset, Duke James's steward, wrote to his absent master. "The young gentleman seems to be good-natured, but I do not think he hath very much in him." Such was D'Eguilles's impression also. Surface charm, a dazzling smile, the graciousness and courtesy of the fated Stuarts—he had all these, but was he a judge of character, one who could deal with older men and mould them to his purpose?

The women? Bah! D'Eguilles, accustomed to the corrupt French court, where the Pompadour continued to hold the King in her toils and sway the destinies of those whom she favoured, watched, with cynical interest, the fair ones who flocked to the evenings at Holyrood. Music, dancing, presentations to the slim young man who for so brief a space reigned there, but the Prince himself looked with an absent eye upon these charmers. The Frenchman recalled a passage in one of his letters to the French ministers. "In general, all the young and pretty women are Jacobites, and the most of them are only such since the arrival of the young Prince. It is not that he is coquettish, or a man of gallantry—quite the contary: it is because he is not, that the Scotswomen, who are naturally serious and impassioned, conclude of him that he is really tender, and will remain constant. It is a woman who has given me this explanation, but be this as it may, it is certain that the friendship of the ladies is not the least powerful force for his party."

The Frenchman, experienced, silent, watched the currents and cross-currents, studied the shoals and quicksands, and saw the rocks and rapids ahead. Well, it had ended, or was tending to end, much as he had all along foreseen. Nevertheless, even at this stage, there might be a faint hope of postponing the inevitable if only the Prince would hear reason——

"*En bien, monsieur le Marquis?*" Charles began.

"Sir, I have begged that your Royal Highness will be graciously pleased to grant me a quarter of an hour's private audience."

"You have it, *monsieur*. We are private—for fifteen minutes."

"Then, sir—— I implore—— I entreat——"

"Two of your fifteen minutes are gone."

"I am here, sir, to ask that you will decline battle with the Duke of Cumberland."

"Refuse to fight? Never!"

"Sir, consider your situation. You are still without half your army."

"Those who have gone to Inverness in quest of food will rejoin directly they learn that the enemy is marching to attack us."

"But those are not all, sir. Others of your force are scattered and cannot arrive in time."

"Cluny and his MacPhersons are on their way from Badenoch. At any minute they should reach us. As for Lord Cromarty, and the Frasers under the Master of Lovat, I anticipate their appearance directly."

Charles's tone was haughty, confident. He looked at the gesticulating figure of the Frenchman and smiled. D'Eguilles recommenced his arguments.

"A great part of those who are available, sir, are without targes. How can they fight with advantage, lacking such a defensive weapon?"

"If you had seen them at Gladsmuir and Falkirk, you would not doubt their fighting qualities." The Prince's head lifted proudly.

"Both times when your Royal Highness won your earlier victories, sir, your army was fresh, well fed, untried. To-day all is vastly different. They are worn out with fatigue after the long march made the previous night."

"Am I rested and refreshed?"

"Sir, I throw myself at your feet. For two days many of them have not eaten at all for want of bread."

The proud lips quivered.

"My steward besought me to eat and had cooked meat for me. Could I feast whilst my Highlanders starve? We are all in the same plight, *monsieur*."

The Frenchman was silent. To beat down that rocklike obstinacy seemed hopeless.

"If we do not fight, what, pray, do you propose instead?" The tone was light, sarcastic.

"Would your Royal Highness consent to fall back to defend Inverness?"

Charles's stubborn silence gave sufficient answer.

"It might be more prudent to abandon the town, sir, and place between the enemy and ourselves the river near which Inverness is built."

The Prince shrugged his shoulders. His full under-lip was thrust out, indicating dissent, disagreement.

The Marquis redoubled his arguments.

"If the worst came to the worst, sir, we might betake ourselves to the neighbouring mountains. There your Royal Highness would be truly invincible." His excitement grew. "There we would remain masters of that part of the coast at which supplies of arms and of money ought to be arriving——"

"Such as those in the *Hazard,* eh, *monsieur le marquis?*" The Prince ground out the words between locked teeth.

"That, sir, was intensely regrettable, most deeply to be deplored."

"Well, continue, pray. Allowing that supplies do arrive——"

"As soon as these reach us, sir, we should march towards England by that same coast as has already been arranged. The more the enemy should advance towards us the greater would be their difficulty to retrace their steps so as to get between ourselves and London. The capture of that great city should be made your Royal Highness's one object, for successes which you might achieve elsewhere would have no decisive value, while, in a single hour, all would be lost without hope of recovery if you should chance to be beaten."

The last word fell drearily into the silence of the room like a lost wind crying over great mountains.

"Beaten?" whispered the Prince.

"Sir, you must face the hazard of it. If you should fail——"

The storm broke and Du Boyer, Marquis D'Eguilles, titular ambassador of the French court, bowed before it.

"Beaten? Fail? Never! Never!" The Prince's voice was almost a scream. "I am resolved to fight at any cost."

"In that event, sir, I beg for your Royal Highness's permission to withdraw to Inverness. My papers must be destroyed with all speed. They cannot be allowed to fall into the enemy's hands."

CHAPTER XIII

THE PRINCE WALKED SLOWLY OUT INTO THE MISTY MORNING. His temples throbbed and everything before his eyes swayed and receded. He felt insulted, outraged, betrayed. That insolent Frenchman! Intolerable! How dared he hint at the possibility, nay, the likelihood of defeat? The idea was fantastic, incredible. Charles's hands clenched. Even to withdraw before the advancing army stung his pride. He must fight. As at Gladsmuir and at Falkirk his men, terrible with dirk and broadsword, would rush upon the foe, mow down the vermin, and re-establish their Prince as victor. He went forward to where his horse awaited him, mounted, and signed briefly to those who were standing by that they were to follow him.

In the saddle his body felt curiously light and weak. After the ordeal of the night-march, its long-drawn-out fatigue and alarms, he had snatched a brief rest, lying, fully dressed and in his boots, on a bed, but he did not sleep, and his only sustenance had been a morsel of bread and a little whisky. He knew that he had never, as he often realized, fully regained his strength after that brief, disastrous illness at Elgin in the previous month, but this day, when so much depended upon steadiness of eyes, firmness of will, it was galling to be shorn of his full physical powers. Hitherto he had scarcely heeded the cold, but this grey April morning it seemed to strike home, to numb him, mentally and bodily, and he found himself shrinking from the snell wind, the occasional particles of sleet falling deliberately out of the leaden sky, and the raw, sodden air which made everything damp and spongy. For a second a longing seized him for the burning sun of Italy, or the fair, springing fields of France, warmth, security, safety, comfort, in place of this bleak, wan north and the constant anxiety, struggle, peril, and effort which had been his portion ever since that fatal landing. Then he straightened his shoulders and lifted his long chin. Bah! He must be light-headed from fasting and weary after the endless night-march, culminating in no useful issue. This was, it should be, the day of third and final victory. Those who spoke of defeat, who even harboured the idea, were cowards, little better than traitors.

Everywhere he could not fail to discern signs of disorder and incomplete preparations. Men, their eyes gummy with sleep, their limbs swaying under them, were being roused mercilessly where they had lain down, overcome by hunger and exhaustion, and herded towards the long plain upon which he had reviewed his army the previous day. Officers galloped past, saluting him hastily, as they made for the open country and even Inverness to round up stragglers and fugitives. The whole scene was one of hurry and futile effort. He rode towards the plateau and found O'Sullivan forming the ranks in order of battle. An atmosphere of disapproval and criticism on the officers' part and weary apathy and resignation on that of the clans overhung everything. A mean rain was beginning to fall.

He galloped down the ranks. A feeble cheer greeted him, but there was no heart or certainty underlying it. The pipes were playing, and for the first time the sound tore at his nerves, rasping them unbearably. He thought of the blazing heat that August day at Glenfinnan and the earliest distant pipe-notes which had heralded the Camerons' coming after hours of suspense and anxiety. Here all was grey, hopeless, and in the watching faces he read neither eagerness nor enthusiasm. The ground was damp and sticky.

Irritably he muttered: "How long they are taking!"

Certain of his officers came up and spoke to him. He answered vaguely, listlessly. Lord George Murray, grim-faced executive, having apparently thrown off his fatigue, was arguing hotly with O'Sullivan. There ensued a dispute about some park walls. Lord Ogilvy's men were being marched off in a particular direction and Lord Ogilvy himself, a boyish bridegroom, looked distinctly sulky. Charles hated to meet Elcho's mocking stare. They were all against him, opposed to him. His decision to fight—the only right step—was disapproved of by everyone. It was cruel, when he risked as much, nay more, than did the rest. He roused himself from his sour reverie as the three MacDonald chiefs—Keppoch, Lochgarry, and Clanranald—approached him.

"Sir, we are come to beg that your Royal Highness will grant us our ancient privilege to-day."

"And that, Keppoch?"

"The honour of the right wing for the MacDonalds, sir."

"Have you not it?" Oh! these clan-customs, clan-rights, clan-jealousies!

"Lord George Murray claims it for his Atholl men, sir."

The Prince sighed and hunched his shoulders.

"I cannot decide in an affair of which I am ignorant, gentlemen. You and my Lord George must settle it amongst yourselves."

What did it matter, a trifle such as this, when a throne, nay, life itself, stood at stake? He realized languidly that a great dispute seemed to be going on, the three MacDonalds arguing and gesticulating, Lord George hard-faced, adamant, but he would not interfere. Lochiel addressed him, explaining that the Murrays claimed to have had the position on the right wing in battle since Montrose's wars, but the Prince brushed him aside. It was of no moment.

"Sir—pardon me!—it is vastly important. The Mac-Donalds will feel themselves slighted, even insulted, and the clansmen will not fight."

"Lochiel! At a time like this to dispute such a trifle, to be aggrieved for nothing! Pah!"

"To Highlanders it is a good deal more than a trifle, sir."

"But what can I do? If I refuse it to Lord George Murray and the Atholl men they will be equally stubborn. I decline to decide upon a point of which I am ignorant."

He moved away with a pettish shrug of the shoulders. Lochiel, he realized, looked after him sorrowfully. What did it matter? Nothing mattered save this creeping cold, the lowering sense of futility and failure, the fierce inner determination to be victorious against the hated foe, and to prove himself right. How thin the long, straggling ranks looked! If he had not dissipated his forces in vain endeavours to reduce far-off strongholds such as Blair Castle and Fort William he would have had many more men to pit against the Duke of Cumberland. It was intolerable that word of the urgency of the situation had not reached the scattered clansmen. Cluny should have had ample time to arrive from Badenoch. Lord Cromarty's delay became inexplicable. He recognized a handful of Frasers, but the Master of Lovat was not with them. Rain dripped sullenly, remorselessly. He remembered that dark evening of wind and storm at Falkirk and the fleeing foe. It must, it should be, the same now. Defeat was incredible.

Someone spoke to him. He rode mechanically to take up his position. The enemy was approaching. Too late to retire to the ground on the far side of the river, too late to flee, to hide, to follow the advice which might have been a wiser course. They must make a stand, a defiance, and when the red-coats were close upon them strike the carrion down. The pipes still chanted their shrill song, but in place of triumph he read in those wild notes a wan despair.

CHAPTER XIV

THE SKY WAS GROWING LIGHTER. IAIN MACDONALD STARED UP at the thinning greyness and prayed for the sun, his only timepiece. What hour could it be? His hunger, gnawing, insistent, made him feel lightheaded, and everything was blurred, unstable. He stumbled along, recalling stupidly April mornings on the croft, the constant crying of the sheep, the birds sailing overhead, the smell of fresh-turned earth on a spade, and the cool sharpness of the wind in his face. The air to-day was misty and dank, chilling him, obscuring the far prospect. Vaguely he wondered what was happening at Culloden. Had Tearlach returned? Would there be a battle? Once he had managed to stay his hunger he must go back and strike at the hated men in red coats, but until then his swimming gaze could not discern an enemy, nor his enfeebled arm thrust downwards with a dirk.

Where was food to be had? On all sides there stretched wild, remote, deserted, desolate country, with neither man nor habitation of man to be descried. He found a ruined, roofless hut with a little stream running brown and swift outside and stooped to slake his thirst, but the water, chill and peaty, was cold, unsatisfying. He dragged himself farther, wondering whether it were dream or reality that he heard someone singing. A greening fold of land rose up and beyond he saw a man, huge and ragged, seated on the turf by an open pack. Iain's lurching, unsteady steps quickened. A pedlar, besides his goods for sale, might carry bread.

The man looked up as a stranger approached. He grinned, showing a toothless mouth in a weather-beaten, crafty face. "Give you good day, friend," he called in the Gaelic.

"Good day," Iain mumbled.

"Where are you from?"

"My home is near the Loch of the grey gulls."

"Far from here."

"Do I not know?"

Iain fell, rather than sat down, on the rough ground. His eyes closed.

"Are ye sick or wandering?"

"I am hungry. I have come in search of food."

"There is no town for many miles."

The sound of running water was like a third voice.

"Have you nothing I could eat?"

"I do not sell food."

"Give me a morsel of bread!"

"There is a clachan a mile from here. Walk you to it. They might have meal."

"I cannot struggle so far. In the name of the Good Being, a crust, a bannock!"

"Crusts and bannocks do not grow on furze bushes."

Was the man mocking him, jeering at his need, his misery? Iain dragged himself upright and made a clutch towards the pack.

The pedlar defended it from him.

"Is there food therein? I must have it."

"Nay, you shall not."

"I shall!"

They were like two wild beasts, one striving to grasp the pack and tear it further open, the other struggling to shield his property.

Iain's free hand went to his dirk——

There was a loaf in the pack, a great wedge of creamy cheese, and a bottle of wine. He tore at the food like a ravenous thing. For a time he cared for naught, heeded naught, save the satisfying of his long hunger. The wine ran down his throat in a warm torrent. As he flung away the empty bottle he felt revived, renewed, a man again, not a shell, a husk, a weak, starving body. What lucky chance had guided his steps to where the pedlar chanced to be? The pedlar——

He lay very still, in a curiously contorted, unnatural attitude. His gnarled hands, out-flung, seemed as though they appealed for—what? Iain crawled to his feet. His brain was clear again. At Gladsmuir and at Falkirk he had seen dead men. He knew that the pedlar was dead—dead, with Iain's dirk in his throat.

A strangled whimper broke from him. What was this that he had done? To kill a man in battle, to slay those who were against Tearlach was, his chief insisted, a right, a glorious thing to do, but the pedlar was no red-coat. He had died at Iain MacDonald's hand in a sordid squabble over food. Iain had murdered him.

What could he do now? By this deed he had made himself an outlaw for ever from decent men. He might be hanged for it. His brain worked blindly, furiously. Was it too late to find his way back to Drummossie? Would his clan hide him? Who was the pedlar? Had he been a wandering figure, going from croft to clachan, from town to village with his pack and his singing and his news? Would he be missed, inquired for, traced to this still thing crushing the moss and turf, and a hue-and-cry arise for his slayer? Iain began to shiver. This spot, seeming so remote and empty, was suddenly peopled with dread and vengeful forms. He must go far from it, no matter whither his steps took him. The body might not be found for many days——

Mairi! He craved to find her, to be once more the tacksman of the little croft, content with simple things, quiet ways. A great surge of anger rose in his breast against the fate which had forced him out and ended in his hands being dyed with blood. He had not meant to kill. The pedlar had brought his end upon himself, grudging a starving man food.

If Tearlach had never come to Scotland! Why should he, a prince, with soft garments and a horse to ride, spoil the lives of poor folk who scarcely knew his name? Iain recalled, scowling, the miseries of the past months, the long marches in every weather, the sullen English faces, the dangers, the cold, the constant hunger and distress. It was not right, no, indeed it was not, that a poor Highland man who earned his bread and tilled his soil and went to kirk and market should leave these things to fight for a young man who would not care whether he were killed, who, in all likelihood, would not know that he had been. They said a battle at Drummossie would decide Tearlach's fate. It could be fought without Iain MacDonald. He would go home—home to Mairi, and if the Prince won, he would not need Iain, and if he were defeated, he could not have him forced out again.

Iain chuckled, weakly, slyly. The wine, strong, an unaccustomed luxury, was mounting to his head. The chuckle changed to a foolish laugh. Och! he was a clever chiel, Iain MacDonald of Keppoch's clan. He was not going to fight for

Tearlach any more. He would go home, and if Keppoch came
again to force him out Iain would tell him that he had done
enough for Tearlach. The rest, the others who stayed to fight
the men the King sent, were fools. When they lay dead—
dead like the pedlar—Iain thrust at the body with his foot—
then Iain would be alive, alive and laughing at them.

He laughed now. The sound frightened him. It was so
thin, so pitiful, in the vast silence, dying away through the
mist like the cry of a child. He began to weep, to stumble
from the spot, to hasten blindly in any direction that might
take him from it. He had killed a man.

The sun should be up by now. He stared at the sky, seeing
nothing save grey clouds, grey vapour. Where was the croft?
The day he was marched off with others of the clan they had
come many long miles. There had been a great river to cross
and everywhere mountains towering in the summer heat. Now
it was cold, cold as that bleak England they had run back
from, and he did not know the road which would lead to
Mairi. He wept more freely, but his tears brought no relief
from fear and loneliness. Why had he left the pedlar's pack
lying behind? It might have held more food. He had eaten
hastily and would soon feel hungry again.

They said that Tearlach was hungry. Iain should have
kept the loaf and taken it back to Drummossie for him. If he
were hungry, how could he fight?

The red-coated men were very strong. Tearlach had lost
many who had fought for him earlier. He would need every
claymore. Iain's unsteady steps halted. Perhaps he ought to
go back. If there was a battle he could kill many of the enemy,
and that might blot out the sin of having slain an unarmed
man. He did not know. Only a blind instinct drove him to
retrace his steps the endless way they had travelled, and a dull
hope that he would be in time to strike at Tearlach's foes kept
him stumbling and running towards where he supposed Drummossie lay.

CHAPTER XV

EDINBURGH WAS GREY AND SWEPT BY A HARSH EAST WIND.
The castle towered against a sky nearly as dark as itself.
The Whigs were again in power, and those brief, mad six
weeks when a Stuart sat in Holyrood seemed to many like a
dream. The Law lord nodded bewigged heads and con-

veniently ignored their own cowardly and abrupt flight from the capital as Charles Edward and his forces advanced. They had saved their skins and their positions, and the blame for the Pretender's temporary successes rested on the shoulders of poltroons like Sir John Cope and Provost Archibald Stewart, or incompetents such as Wade and Hawley. Now Edinburgh Castle held prisoner many of those who had dared to take up arms for the Stuart Cause, and a bitter price most should pay.

Amongst the latter was a Highland chief on whom Fate had played a grim trick. Donald MacDonald of Kinlochmoidart sat in the darkness of his cell, fettered, friendless, forsaken. He was young and strong and ardent and longed to strike another blow on behalf of his dear Prince. How did matters go with Tearlach Og? The Highlander pressed his forehead against the chill stone of the enclosing walls, seeing not the slit of window which framed a grey square of sky, but wide stretches of wine-red moor, heather purple under the sunset's spilled gold, and the blue glance of a long loch. Here, on this sixteenth day of April, 1746, his thoughts were with that brilliant summer morning when he had crossed Loch Lochy on the Prince's business. The previous day his brother Aeneas, almost a stranger, had arrived after the forty-mile journey from Eriska and the two met for the first time in many years. Aeneas had been in the banking business in Paris and had had the Prince under his roof. This much Kinlochmoidart knew, but he had been unprepared for the tidings that Charles was in Scotland, on board a ship anchored off Arisaig. Kinlochmoidart was reckoned cool-headed by his family and contemporaries, but the information sent his caution to the winds. His heart thudding, he accompanied his brother back to the vessel where he laid his sword and his service at Charles's feet. His eyes dimmed, recalling his first sight of the Prince. Even the ugly dress of an ecclesiastic, the rough beard, could not disguise his royalty or dim his good looks. The quick, high voice rang in Kinlochmoidart's ears now. Charles was eager, enthusiastic, sanguine. Oh! it was a great hazard—with bright eyes he acknowledged as much—but it should, it must, succeed. Kinlochmoidart ventured to ask if what his brother told him as to his Royal Highness's support were true. Charles laughed, startling the sea-birds. Yes, he had little money, a scant supply of arms, for which, he admitted, he stood heavily indebted to the good Waters, and only seven followers. Then——

"Nay, do not look so glum, *mon ami*." He clapped his hand on the MacDonald's shoulder. "I expect—I confidently expect—the Highlands to rise. You will bring out your men——"

"With all my power, sir."

"Then the rest will follow."

He was so certain, so secure in his conviction of the rightness of his Cause, so determined to ignore the difficulties ahead, that Kinlochmoidart had not the heart to discourage him. The Prince was very gracious, appointing the new adherent a colonel and aide-de-camp to his Royal Highness. Even now Kinlochmoidart smiled covertly as he recalled Murray of Broughton's transparent jealousy over the coveted position. He would have preferred the post instead of that of secretary to the Prince. Well—the captive shrugged his shoulders wearily—what advantage had the royal favour gained for either? He lay here, a prisoner, with trial and death, in all likelihood, looming before him in the inescapable future, and Murray—— Scraps of news penetrated even these grim walls. Murray was ill, had left the Prince's service. The Jacobite army was, Kinlochmoidart learned, somewhere in the neighbourhood of Inverness, preparing to fight the forces of the Duke of Cumberland. What hope could there be of defeating these seasoned soldiers? His heart grew heavy as he foresaw the inevitable end——

That broiling day, with the sun smiting the deep waters of Loch Lochy. He could feel the heat now although his cell was clammy-cold. The clansmen's strong arms drove the little boat through the waves and another speck upon them resolved itself into a second boat, bearing his kinsman and namesake, Hugh MacDonald of Morar. They hailed one another over the space of water dividing their crafts.

"Give you good day, Hugh."

"Good day to you, Donald."

"What news?"

"No news at all have I."

Across the months he could hear his own laugh. "Then I'll give you news. You'll see the Prince this night."

Hugh MacDonald was excited, yet puzzled. "What Prince do you mean?"

"Prince Charles."

"You are certainly joking."

"I assure you it is true."

"Then what number of men has he brought with him?"

"Only seven."

"What stock of money and arms has he brought with him, then?"

"A very small stock of either."

"What generals or officers fit for commanding are with him?"

"None at all."

Kinlochmoidart had spoken lightly, gaily, the very madness of the venture inspiring him. Hugh MacDonald's face grew longer and more dubious. "I do not like the expedition," he muttered. "I am afraid of the consequences."

The sun had gone suddenly behind a cloud. The waters of the loch were no more sapphire, but a dull grey. A fine film of rain, one of those brief, smiting showers which the Highlands know so well, began to obscure the mountains, and a sea-bird's sharp, fretful wail sounded a note of omen, of doom. Kinlochmoidart shook off his mood and answered bravely.

"If the matter go wrong, then I'll certainly be hanged, for I am engaged already."

A shudder went over him now as he remembered his own words, uttered half-jestingly, yet with an undercurrent of fearful truth beneath. If the venture went wrong——— Ay, it had, and he was caught in the net Fate had woven.

How had it fallen out thus? He lay here, in Edinburgh Castle, the prisoner of the Government, a traitor to the reigning House, and the death traitors died was———

He looked down at his virile, healthy body. Was life to be choked out of it, torn from it, and his head be set upon a gate in an alien town, the sightless eyes gazing towards Scotland? It might not be. The Prince was not yet defeated. He might once again retake the ancient capital of his northern kingdom, fling wide the prison gates, and set the captives free. *Tearlach! Tearlach!*

Well, Kinlochmoidart had served his Prince, though he had never drawn sword in battle for him. His high mood of exaltation fell from him as he remembered his loyal acts and how they had led him to this. Young Clanranald had sailed for Skye and sounded Sir Alexander MacDonald of Sleat and MacLeod of MacLeod. All he had been able to bring back to the Prince was their blunt refusals to come out. Charles had fretted and persisted, declining to take the answers as final. Ultimately he, Kinlochmoidart, had been sent on a similar embassage, to make another appeal. His heart was high, his hopes sanguine, for the Prince was succeeding beyond even his own dreams, and had marched into England. Kinloch-moidart reached Skye and met with the same rejection of his plea as had Clanranald. Frustrated, disappointed, furious with the Skye chiefs' cold caution and MacLeod's half-known treachery, for was not he the gentleman of consequence in the Highlands who had written word of Charles's arrival to the Government and sent President Forbes of Culloden in his boots hot-foot northward, Kinlochmoidart travelled south to rejoin the Prince. Despite his own disappointment at the failure of his mission his hopes were not dimmed. The Prince was heading for London. On the march the English Jacobites would join him and the English cities fall. He pressed forward, attended only by a single servant, Angus M'Pherson. It was November and raw, wintery weather. At mean inns or shabby change-houses he sought for news of the Prince's progress, but what he learned appalled him. Charles was spoken of with indifference more than active dislike or hostility. Over the Border none had joined him beyond a parcel of shabby fellows who did not care whom they served so long as they had food and pay. Kinlochmoidart choked as he remembered his own fierce incredulity, merging into dismay, when he was told that Wade's force, the Duke of Cumberland's, and an army of unknown strength gathered outside London barred the Prince's passage to the throne. He might even be compelled to retreat.

Then let him come back to his own Scotland and she would welcome him. Lord John Drummond, the Duke of Perth's brother, and Lord Strathallan had collected encouraging support, and a considerable army was gathered about Perth and Dunblane. Kinlochmoidart himself would hasten ahead and meet Charles. All could not be lost.

It was a short, bleak, winter day. He was in Lanarkshire, passing through Lesmahago. The air blew raw and chill. The early darkness was beginning to gather. Mounted on rough horses Kinlochmoidart and his servant thrust forward, rode through the village, and emerged into the wild country beyond. There was a waste piece of land, styled Brokencross Muir, a straggling, desolate region, unmarked by light or footfall. It was imperative to find some shelter for the oncoming night as the country was highly hostile to the Prince's Cause. He himself felt uneasy because at the door of the change-house he had noticed a young student of divinity with whom he had a slight acquaintance, an arrant Whig. Absurd to contemplate the youth doing him any harm, but in these times caution was a wise companion.

The damp silence turned his mood to melancholy. Where was the Prince? In what humour would he be after these checks to his high hopes? Was that a dull sound of shouting? He glanced about him uneasily, concluded that he must have been mistaken, and called sharply to his servant to ride faster. Angus M'Pherson answered in the Gaelic that his beast was weary.

"So is mine. Nevertheless, we should not loiter. What was that?"

A horseman had spurred out of the murk. It was the youthful probationer. He had utilized a local short cut, unknown to the two travellers, and was upon them, armed. In the name of the Elector he commanded both to surrender. Behind him, a confused rabble of country folk, armed with old guns and pitchforks, was bearing down upon the pair. The Highland servant unslung his piece.

"A brace of bullets will settle them," he grinned.

"Nay. We must have no bloodshed," Kinlochmoidart had answered.

Never dreaming of the fate that would overtake him, he surrendered. The sallow-faced divinity student had carried him in triumph back to the village, the local population cursing and threatening. He saw the place now, low-roofed, mean houses, a staring, hostile community running to and fro, jeering, exulting, and a dark stream curving alongside the ill-drained street. Under a strong guard he was taken to Edinburgh Castle, and for five months had languished within its walls. His bitterest thought was that he could no longer serve his dear Prince.

CHAPTER XVI

ENOCH BRADSHAW, A SOLDIER IN COBHAM'S DRAGOONS, HAD drunk the Duke of Cumberland's health with acclaim. Billy was the boy for him! Only a few more hours, perhaps, and this interminable waiting, these tedious weeks of inaction and monotony would end in a glorious clash with the rebels. He spat contemptuously. A set of lousy, ill-clad, bare-legged Highlanders, not much better than savages. And their Pretender? Bah! Enoch would like to see him face to face with their Duke. Easy to guess which would show himself the better man.

He came from Gloucestershire, and after the gracious fields, the warm English winds, the hedges and downland and rolling country he looked on Scotland with a jaundiced eye. The women were ugly and unfriendly, the scenery, the farther north the army advanced, wilder and more unfamiliar, the climate enough to kill a horse. He had followed in the tracks of the retreating Highland army and tasted the temper of the north of England towards it. Charles had brought misery on countless people who never saw his face. The rankest Jacobite should be sick of the name of Stuart. He must be utterly defeated and his ragged force scattered or slain. Nor was that enough. He himself needed to be taken prisoner, tried, condemned, and—— Enoch hunched doubtful shoulders. Well, Charles was Billy's cousin and the King—God save him!— might not like to cut off his head, but if a private man, say one Enoch Bradshaw, could be alone with him, it would be his glory to stab the villain to the heart.

Enoch licked thick lips and mused upon the pleasing picture. The last of the Stuart race, it would look well in history for him to fall by the hand of a Bradshaw. The only difficulty was that Charles was too well guarded. The days of being easily accessible to all and sundry had ended. Always he kept his Highlanders about him, or some of those low Irish. Enoch spat again. A parcel of self-seeking, papist dogs! They would run away at the first shot.

Blurred pictures of the army's progress through England into this vile Scotland came to memory. Flat, wet lanes, a dark little spinney, a red sunset over Clifton Moor. Here they had nearly caught up with the rebels, but Billy's cavalry and dismounted dragoons were beaten off by the wretches, a lasting disgrace. Edinburgh had been well enough pleased to see the Duke. It was a pity that the old palace—what was the name of the place? Oh, Linlithgow—should have been set on fire by Billy's men, but it had been a pure accident, and English soldiers needed better accommodation than the crumbling building afforded, and a Scotch winter was so damnably cold that a fire was a necessity. Who could tell that the straw, newly-kindled, would soon be out of control? They said that old kings and queens, Charles's ancestors, had been born there. The people of the town looked sour enough at the conflagration. The Jacobites, though, had got even with Billy's troops.

They blew up the church of St. Ninian. No use to blame the English soldiers there. Eh? Ha! ha!

It was April, but cursedly unlike an English spring. He thought of the ripening fields in Gloucestershire, the squandered yellow of primrose and cowslip, the budding hedges, the gentle winds and soft, fine rain. Here a man was chilled and frozen, wading waist-deep through snow-swollen rivers, or camping with a vile east wind blowing sleet or hail in his face. The very speech of the inhabitants rang harsh and uncouth. Their food was only fit for pigs.

Nevertheless, this victory should be worth waiting for and could not be long delayed. Enoch grinned to himself. Billy left nothing to chance. He had spies, speaking the uncouth Gaelic tongue and wearing the outlandish Highland garb, who mixed with the rebels on their night-march to Nairn, and took the opportunity to slip away at different times and bring the Duke notice of their progress. The last of them, one Shaw, came with intelligence before dawn. He was closeted with Billy for some time and Enoch would have given a share of his pay to know what passed between them. There could be no question of the rebels attacking. Captain Hall, in command of a party of dragoons, patrolled all night between the River Nairn and the sea, and to the west of the camp, between the King's army and the Highlanders—lousy dogs!—were the Argyllshire men, commanded by Colonel Campbell. They said he was like to be Duke of Argyll some day.

Hard on Shaw's visit there came orders to the men to lie down and take some rest. They were to have their arms by them. He slept soundly, despite the cursed cold. His dreams were a medley of past and future. Bess, the red-lipped dairymaid from Shooters' Farm, was kissing him behind a haystack. If he came out of this he might marry Bess when he got home. Her plump, warm body, her ready mouth were better worth having than the stiff Scotch girls who looked at an honest English soldier as though he were some unclean animal. Enoch chuckled. He and John Arkwright of Pulteney's and one or two others had taught that yellow-headed wench in Aberdeen a thing or two. She had screamed loudly enough to bring the Town Council out of their beds, but it availed her nothing. Ho! ho!

A bugle call. The drums were beating. He sprang up, fully awake, his heart thumping a shade faster than its wont. Here was the day of victory when Billy should wipe out the stain of Fontenoy, teach the Scotch a lesson, and send the Pre-

tender packing. Where? Enoch pondered this, grinning.
Back to the Continent, lousy with Papists like himself? The
King of France would be pleased to have him home and give
him one of his daughters, most likely. Or the Pope of Rome,
only he hadn't any daughters, none, that was to say, as he could
acknowledge. A good jest that. He must remember it to tell
Jerry Mole of Bligh's. Jerry liked a laugh.

It would be fairly bad luck if any of his friends were killed
to-day. Even half-starved and ill-equipped those dogs of Highlanders could fight. They told gory tales of Gladsmuir when
the poor English soldiery were mown down by their uncouth
weapons and Johnny Cope ran away as fast as his legs would
carry him. Charles had won there.

Falkirk must not be forgotten either. Hawley had put
up a mighty poor show. They said he was actually wasting his
time with some fine lady, a countess, when a message came that
the Pretender's army was marching, and off he rode, but it
was not much use. Of course the weather had been against
him. Rain and wind in his men's faces gave the damned Scots
a better chance. No such luck was going to avail them this
day, please God. Billy would see to that.

What a country! What a climate! In Gloucestershire the
apple and pear blossom would be making the orchards as if a
shower of snow had fallen over them, and the trees would all
be green, but here this dreary landscape spread for miles
with nothing save sheep-nibbled turf, clumps of furze, and on
the branches only hard little buds. It was as cold as mid-
winter. He felt its bite even through his thick clothing as
he ate the ample breakfast provided. Billy knew that a man
needed a full stomach before he faced his enemy. Those
stinking Highlanders would have empty bellies. It was talk
in the camp that they had had only a biscuit apiece all yesterday. Charles was no general. Small wonder that the men he
commanded slipped away whenever they saw a chance. He
was a soft-hearted fool, too. He let them go instead of fetching
them back. If Billy's soldiers dared to desert——

He was standing at the door of his tent now. A bit on the
portly side, but erect, soldierly, his hard blue eyes roaming
everywhere, his glance alert to detect anything amiss. Enoch
saw him beckon to one of his officers and from the way the
fellow bowed and retreated, red to the ears, when Billy had
finished speaking to him, he had had a good piece of the royal
mind. That was what the men liked, though. They did not
get all the blame. The officers had to be ready to shoulder

any responsibility, the soldiers to obey orders, and, dang it!
with Billy to give the orders every man was itching to carry
them out and be at the rebels' throats.

The house where the Pretender lodged looked a fine building. When they had the Scotch beaten perhaps the victorious
soldiers might be allowed to loot a little. He should like to
bring Bess back something from Scotland which would cause
her round blue eyes to bolt and her mouth to open with surprise and delight. Poor Bess! She had cried the night he went
to tell her that he was ordered to Scotland, and how warm
and soft her body had felt in his arms. She did not like his
going so far, she whimpered. The Highlanders were savages.
They might never see each other again. Women were poor
creatures. She could not understand the glory of it, his meagre
share in making Billy victorious over the rebels.

He hoped that he would not be killed. It was a poor end
for a Bradshaw to have his throat slit by one of their outlandish weapons. Enoch grinned afresh. Billy had seen the
danger in the way the kilted dogs fought. He had urged the
use of the bayonet and made his men practise a different style
of fighting. Before this the bayonet-man attacked the sword-
man right fronting him. Now the left-hand bayonet attacked
the sword fronting his next right-hand man. He was then
covered by the enemy's shield where open upon his left, and
the enemy's right open to him. This, Billy argued, would
make an essential difference, stagger the enemy, who would not
be prepared to alter their way of fighting, and destroy them
in a manner sooner to be conceived than told. Oh! Billy was
every inch a soldier, God bless him, and if he, Enoch Bradshaw,
fell to-day it would be at Billy's orders and to defend England
from the rebel curs.

William Augustus, Duke of Cumberland, rode through the
grey morning. It was hard upon eleven o'clock, yet still
misty, dark, sunless, with the threat of rain growing hourly.
His trained eye ranged over the forces under his command. At
five a.m. they had assembled, been given a substantial breakfast, and then received the order to march. They were formed
into five lines each of three battalions, headed by Major-
General Huske on the left, Brigadier Sempill on the right, and
Brigadier Mordaunt in the centre. The horse, under General
Hawley and General Bland, flanked them, and at the same
time covered the cannon on the right and left.

For eight miles the long columns marched steadily. The
ground was boggy and marshy, the air cold, nipping, easterly.

Suddenly, out of the mist and uncertainty ahead, he heard
voices. A young aide-de-camp galloped up. The Duke turned
in his saddle.

"Well, Captain Conway?"

The messenger saluted briskly.

"Sir, the detachment of Kingston's Horse, forty of whom
your Royal Highness sent in advance of the army, together
with the Argyllshire Highlanders, to discover the rebels'
motions, report that their van is moving towards us."

"Ha!"

"The army awaits your Royal Highness's directions, sir."

The great moment was at hand. Curtly Cumberland barked
his orders.

"The three battalions of the second line defile to the left
of the battalions in the van. Barrel's to the left of Munro's,
Scots fusiliers to the left of Price's, and Chomondeley's to the
left of the Royals."

It was nearly midday. Enoch Bradshaw heard an officer,
after consulting his repeater, call this out to Captain Hard-
castle of Sempill's. His trained countryman's eye judged the
distance from the ground where the rebels were drawn up in
order of battle to be about two miles. The King's troops
formed in two lines: three regiments for the reserve, the
cavalry on the left flank, the most exposed position, the right
secured by a morass. Enoch's nose wrinkled. He did not fancy
a roll in that boggy patch of ground and a Highlander's dirk in
his gizzard immediately afterwards. To the left there rose
an eminence, scarcely to be called a hill. The best clans of the
rebels were endeavouring to gain it. This did not accord with
Billy's plan. He made a movement to the left and secured the
top of the hill as soon as the kilted vermin. It was easy to see
that this disconcerted them a good deal. Finding that they were
outflanked on the right by Billy's left they changed their dispositions and attempted to bring up troops from their second
line to fall upon Billy's right flank.

The morass was ended. Enoch glanced uneasily around.
The right flank was quite uncovered to the enemy. Billy at
once gave sharp orders. Kingston's Horse was to come from the
reserve, and a little squadron of Cobham's, including Enoch,
and some sixty other men, who had been patrolling, to cover
the flank. Pulteney's regiment was summoned from the reserve
to the right of the Royals. This secures us entirely on that side,
Enoch chuckled to himself.

They had advanced until the rebels were only some five

hundred yards away. The enemy had begun to cannonade the King's troops with their few toy pieces of cannon. A return fire disconcerted them, but they continued to advance. Enoch chuckled. The lads fought more like devils than like men. The kilted terrors were flinging themselves on the front line, breaking through Barrel's and Munro's regiments, but their success was brief. Wolfe's regiment was advancing and entirely defeated their design. General Hawley and Major-General Bland, with the portion of the cavalry posted on the left, had broken down some park walls which the Highlanders flattered themselves covered their right wing. It could not be long now——

Billy's words, as he rode along the lines, speaking to every battalion, ay, almost to every platoon, rang in Enoch's ears still. "Depend, my lads, on your bayonets. Let them mingle with you; let them know the men they have to deal with." Well, they soon would, and then—— No quarter. Ha! ha! No quarter.

CHAPTER XVII

THE PRINCE SAT ON HORSEBACK ON A LITTLE EMINENCE FROM which the entire Highland army was under his eye. He still felt semi-dazed, as though the events taking place so swiftly were some ill dream. The rain-sodden tartans, the blurred hues of plaid and kilt, swam before him. The skirling of the pipes was a growing torture. He was glad when they sank to silence and the monotonous rumble of musketry took their place. His own guns, feeble, few, ineffective, were speaking, answering the enemy's sterner fire. Why did the Highlanders not charge? Were they to stand there, cannon-balls making havoc in their meagre numbers, whilst they waited, dumbly patient, for Lord George Murray to give the order which should unleash their straining ranks?

The mist, half rain, was thick and clouded with particles of powder. He peered through it, his eyes straining to pick out the different clans. Lord Ogilvy's Angus battalion in the reserve, in the first line the Atholl men, Camerons, Stewarts of Appin, Frasers, Mackintoshes, Farquharsons, MacLeans, Mac-Lachlans, MacLeods, Chisholms; the second line, Glenbucket's men, all remaining of the Scottish cavalry, the French Picquets, Fitzjames's Horse, others he could not distinguish—they were there, together with the MacDonalds, that solid wedge on the left. His teeth caught at his underlip. By this time he had learned what a stubborn value the Highlanders set on their clan privileges. The MacDonalds claimed the right wing in battle since the Bruce gave the distinction to a MacDonald ancestor. Ah! but Lord George—a murrain on his sullen face!—swore that since Montrose's wars the Atholl Murrays enjoyed this privilege. His, the Prince's, ought to have been the deciding voice, but he was too weary, too hungry, too dazed with fatigue and lack of food, to intervene, to listen to angry argument and counter-argument, and in the end to disoblige the one who lost the casting vote. What did such a little thing matter? Let all fight for their Prince, their honour, and the fate of Scotland.

Why did the waiting ranks not charge? Already he could discern gaps where the enemy's fire had found its mark. Gladsmuir . . . Falkirk. As in a dream he remembered his first victory. It had been September, a cloudless, warm day in an unbroken succession of such days. The Forth lay blue and clear and the long harvest fields slanted golden under the sunset. He rode out from Holyrood to Duddingston and there took up his quarters. What a vivid time it had been, sending reconnaissance parties to discover the enemy's strength and motions, setting his own forces in order of battle, issuing instructions to his officers, arranging for surgeons from Edinburgh to be in readiness, and procuring carriages for the conveyance of the wounded after the battle. The still night wore on. The noisy, incessant barking of dogs in Tranent village was the only sound. A creeping mist dimmed the red glow of Cope's camp fires, and frost tinged the air. He himself had slept in the open field, soundly, dreamlessly, with the pease-straw for mattress and a white greatcoat as covering. Lord George had wakened him, with Anderson of Whitburgh. They brought news of the path across the bog. Then had come the silent advance, and in the misty darkness, two hours before sunrise, Cope mistook the long files of Highlanders for a hedge and lost all advantage. It had been a cheap, easy victory. Afterwards followed the second triumphal entry into Edinburgh and his brief reign there. Falkirk, too, was another success, but to-day—to-day——

Ha! the clans were moving at last. Those must be the Mackintoshes, thrusting forward, hurling themselves upon the ranks of Cumberland's men. They had pierced the first line. Its massed solidity wavered, backed, seemed as though it were cut through. He trained his eyes. The mist was thickening and the wind blew the smoke of grape-shot and powder directly in his face. He could discern nothing distinctly. Now for a further charge by the entire army, the fierce, relentless cutting down of the red-coats. If all the clans followed the Mackintoshes' lead——

He stared about him, peering through the murk. Why were the MacDonalds standing motionless? They had made no attempt to advance, remaining stiff, immobile, like pawns upon a chess-board. He descried a figure—Keppoch? Lochgarry?—arguing, gesticulating, obviously pleading with them to forget their grievance, but his urging was useless. They did not stir, and—ah, *mon Dieu!*—the clans which had broken Cumberland's front line and flung themselves upon the second were being mown down, driven back, scattered, slain. Did his eyes see truly? It was like a dream, a fantastic nightmare, a happening that could not be reality. What now? What now?

A hand was tugging at his bridle. Someone strove to turn his horse's head. He beat at the hand and cried aloud that he would not move. Voices clamoured in his ear, entreating him to come, not to delay, to ride with all speed from the scene. At first he strove to break free, to rally the fleeing and disordered clans, but vainly. They closed about him, men with haggard faces and grim mouths, one thing only in their minds, their Prince's safety. At any second a stray musket shot might find in him its victim. Come, come, oh, come!

He rode, crouching low in the saddle, from the scene of carnage. Was he indeed defeated as many had foretold? Whose was the blame? Could he not turn and order the clans to reform and charge? The sleet was growing thicker. It blinded him until everything swam in a wild phantasmagoria. He saw only a blurred landscape, dim shapes of mountains, stern, harsh faces of men who galloped with him, and behind death, destruction, and despair. This was truly the end of all his fair hopes. Why had his friends forced him from the field? Better, ah! far better to have fallen leading the clans, than to ride away seeking his own safety, and at the mercy of every foe.

One last incident stamped itself upon his reeling mind. A huge fellow, wearing the MacDonald tartan, was laying blindly about him and had accounted for several of the foe before being slaughtered himself. Charles recalled him vaguely. He never forgot a face and the man, one of Keppoch's MacDonalds, had brought Keppoch a message when he was with his Prince, and Charles had made the clansman happy by a passing smile.

CHAPTER XVIII

IT WAS EARLY AFTERNOON, BUT THE OVERHANGING MIST AND clouded skies caused it to seem later than it really was. So reflected Lady Ogilvy, Lord Ogilvy's young bride, as she stood yawning at the window of a house out by Inverness. All along the weather had been strange—grey, sunless, springless, cheerless. Would anybody think it April?

Her meditations were interrupted by the entrance of Lady Gordon and the latter's kinswoman, Lady Kinloch. All three were confident of a Jacobite victory. In anticipation of this they were attending a ball to celebrate the event later in the evening. Lady Gordon did not propose to dance, being in a delicate state of health, but she vowed that nothing should rob her of witnessing the spectacle and kissing the victor's royal hand. After greetings, an eager discussion as to the dress each lady intended to wear broke out.

"Margaret must appear in her wedding-gown," declared Lady Kinloch. "Do you not agree, Janet?"

"Entirely, ma'am. There's nothing so becoming to her."

"I wore it at Holyrood," objected Lady Ogilvy. "I vow everybody must be sick of the sight of it."

"Holyrood!" sighed Lady Gordon. "Ah! what a bonnie spectacle that would have been. And your ladyship danced there, of course?"

"With my spouse, ma'am."

"La! Not with the Prince?"

"His Royal Highness, you'll remember, declined dancing whilst in Edinburgh. He used to say when he returned from England, victorious, he should give a ball and dance then."

"He has danced here," murmured Lady Kinloch. "We have had several balls, and he was graciously pleased to lead me out at more than one."

"His feet may have danced, but his heart was not in the diversion, ma'am."

All three ladies sighed. Well they knew that the situation of the Prince's affairs was far from prosperous, but to-day might see a change. He was certain of a victory over the Duke of Cumberland. They must not allow themselves to grow doleful.

"What hour is it?" Lady Kinloch inquired.

"Past three o'clock, ma'am. Do you think a dish of tea would hearten us?"

"An admirable suggestion of your ladyship's."

Lady Ogilvy pulled the bell-rope and a rough servant-lass appeared. Tea was ordered and duly brought in. The three ladies sipped and chattered. Outwardly they appeared cheerful and unconcerned, but privately each was anxious and harassed. What was happening at Culloden? Had Cumberland marched? Were the husbands of all three safe? How of the Prince? Each, securely and satisfactorily married, had handed over a portion of her heart to the fascinating youthful adventurer who had set Scotland in such a stir. His safety, his success were of paramount importance. Bonnie Prince Charlie!

"Was that a knock?" Lady Ogilvy's white hand, holding the teapot, shook slightly.

There was a swirl of skirts, a laughing voice, and Colonel Ann, as the Jacobites dubbed Lady Mackintosh ever since her successful ruse had prevented the Prince from being taken prisoner at Moy, swept into the room. For a wife whose husband was with the Government, and whose clan in defiance of him she had brought out for the Cause, she seemed remarkably carefree and gay. There were greetings, exclamations, questions.

"Ann!"

"Margaret!"

"Janet, my sweet friend!"

"My dearest Lady Mackintosh!"

"And how does my Lady Kinloch?"

"Ma'am, your servant!"

"Pray sit down, Ann, and take a cup of tea with us."

"I am monstrous thirsty," Ann Mackintosh confessed.

"And—what news?"

Lady Mackintosh's mouth—a very pretty one—drooped.

"Positively none, my dear. There cannot have been any battle. As I rode here I saw a few Highlanders, but they seemed to be seeking bread."

"Ah! then there is no fighting?"

"Rely upon it, that had there been these men would have stayed beside the Prince."

"I wish we could hear something," sighed Lady Ogilvy.

The rest exchanged commiserating glances. Poor Margaret! So recently wed and her young bridegroom separated from her, sharing the perils and hazards of the Prince's enterprise. No wonder that she felt dowie. To cheer her Lady Mackintosh introduced the fascinating subject of clothes.

"I have brought my gown for to-night's diversion. Would you ladies advise me?'

"Oh, with vast pleasure, Ann. But are you not satisfied with it? These mantua-makers——"

"'Tis the shoulder-knot," confessed Lady Mackintosh. "My mother-in-law and I cannot agree whether the ribbon should be of the Stuart or the Mackintosh tartan."

The others gazed at Lady Mackintosh. Here was indeed a problem!

"Which do you incline to?" inquired Lady Ogilvy.

"Can you ask? Our beloved Prince's colours, of course, but I dislike to disoblige my mother-in-law."

"Especially when she has had the honour of his Royal Highness actually lodging under her roof. Ah! what happiness!" sighed Janet Gordon.

"You had better wear the Mackintosh tartan as a shoulder-knot, ma'am." Lady Kinloch, the oldest lady present, gave the casting vote. "Would it not be possible to contrive a smaller one of Stuart tartan for the corsage, or to sport a white cockade?"

"Ma'am, I vow you have the happiest ideas. I shall most certainly do that," declared Colonel Ann.

"Do not let us forget the time, ladies."

"Perhaps we had better dress now," Lady Ogilvy suggested.

The ball was to be held at the house of a neighbouring laird whose wife was hotly Jacobite. Margaret Ogilvy attired herself for it with flushed cheeks and tremulous lips. Surely her husband would come, nay, certainly the Prince himself. The event was to celebrate his triumph over his enemies. Then—then, pray God peace again, and the wedded life so sadly interrupted might be taken up afresh. Truly—the young bride waxed indignant—she had scarce seen her spouse since he brought his sword to the Prince at Perth. They had gone to Edinburgh together, where he was in command of the Ogilvys, but—her ladyship pouted—it had been all drilling and marching and orders and counter-orders and her husband one of the Prince's council and mighty important, with scant leisure for his wife. Why, on the march into England she was obliged to content herself with the company of Mrs. Murray of Broughton, wife of the Prince's secretary, who had made herself far too conspicuous distributing white cockades at the Mercat Cross in Edinburgh. At this point Lady Ogilvy's conscience reminded her that she herself had stood upon the Cross of Coupar in Angus, a drawn sword in her hand, whilst the Prince was proclaimed, but that was at her husband's orders. My Lord Ogilvy, though not neglectful, was far too much taken up with this man's business of the Rising.

She looked very bonnie to-night. Her David would dance with her and whisper how dearly he loved her. Nay, even the Prince himself might partner her in reel or strathspey. She turned to take up her fan——

"Margaret! Oh, Margaret!"

"Janet! What is amiss?"

Lady Gordon had burst into the room. Vastly unmannerly of her not to knock! What ailed her? Her head was only partly dressed and one shoe was missing. She wailed her friend's name.

"Janet, are you ill?"

"I would I were dead," wept Lady Gordon.

"But—— But—— Oh, speak! Is it your husband—or—mine?"

Lady Gordon sobbed uncontrollably.

"Janet"—Margaret Ogilvy gripped her by the shoulder—"if you do not tell me what is amiss I shall scream. Have pity!"

"Margaret, 'tis the Prince—the poor Prince."

"And—— What of him? Has he fallen sick again?"

"No. They are saying below—Mungo, the piper, came in. He told of a battle earlier in the day near Culloden."

"A battle? Is Cumberland defeated?"

"Nay. The Prince is."

Lady Ogilvy shrieked faintly. The room swayed round her. Her waiting-woman whimpered in a corner. Candles flared on discarded jewellery and tossed articles of rich attire. Outside, a rising wind whined. It was growing dark.

"Charles—defeated?" whispered Margaret Ogilvy.

"Yes."

"Then—— Our husbands? Janet!"

"Woe! Woe! Wae's me!"

"The Cause?"

"Lost! Lost!"

"Someone is knocking. It may be other news. Mungo is fond of a dram. He—he heard a rumour and ran here."

"No. Those were soldiers."

They stood, whey-faced, clinging to one another. A thunderous hammering on the house door shattered the silence.

"Where are Lady Kinloch and Ann?" whispered Lady Ogilvy.

"They were attiring themselves for the ball. A ball! And now—this!" Lady Gordon tittered hysterically.

It seemed hours before the bedroom door was flung open unceremoniously. A stout, red-faced Hanoverian officer stood on the threshold. Something in his glance made Lady Ogilvy snatch up a cloak and hide her bare neck and shoulders.

"To what do we owe the honour of this—intrusion, sir?" she demanded coldly.

Major Cheeseman of Lord Mark Kerr's Dragoons bowed clumsily.

"Your name, ma'am?"

"I am Margaret Ogilvy, sir, wife to David, Lord Ogilvy, the Earl of Airlie's son and heir."

He nodded curtly.

"And yours, ma'am?" he snapped at Lady Gordon.

"Janet Gordon, sir. I am wife to Sir William Gordon of Park."

"Are you indeed, ma'am? Then let me tell you"—his little eyes flashed angrily—"that you are wedded to a d——d rebel. 'Tis well known that Gordon of Park joined that other rebel, old Pitsligo, after the rout at Gladsmuir, and has served the Pretender throughout his campaign."

Her slender figure straightened. "As have all loyal men —and women, sir."

The crimson deepened in the officer's weather-scalded face.

"Well, let me inform your ladyships that you are both my prisoners."

There was a long silence. A curtain swayed in the draught caused by the open door. Beyond it a file of soldiers could be discerned.

"Your prisoners?" whispered Margaret Ogilvy.

"I presume that you aren't deaf, ma'am. My prisoners is what I said."

"Then—is it true?" faltered Lady Gordon.

"Is what true?"

"That—the battle—went against—him?"

"Whom? The Young Pretender? Certainly 'tis true, my lady. A fine drubbing we gave the rebels this forenoon, I can assure you."

Lady Gordon moaned faintly. Lady Ogilvy stood with her hands pressed over her mouth. At length she let them fall. "And the Prince?" she asked calmly.

"The Pretender your ladyship means?"

"No, sir. I alluded to his Royal Highness, the Prince Regent."

"There's no such person, ma'am. Charles Edward Stuart was defeated by the Duke of Cumberland, in command of His Majesty's forces, and I regret that I en't in a position to inform you of the Young Pretender's present whereabouts."

"You mean, sir, that he is dead?"

"Not he, my lady. Rode off to save his skin directly he saw our men driving the rebel dogs back."

"God keep him!" muttered Lady Gordon.

"You do not seem greatly concerned for your spouses, the pair of you." Major Cheesemen's portly person shook with a series of odious chuckles. "Has Charlie seduced your affections away from your lawful husbands, eh?"

"Your jesting is in mighty poor taste, sir."

"I spoke in earnest, ma'am. 'Tis well known that the Pretender professes to be cold to the petticoats, but he has turned all their heads. The ladies, if you will except one or two, became passionately fond of the young adventurer, and used all their arts and industry for him in the most intemperate manner. There was a pretty tale of a black-browed b—— in Glasgow, one Walkinshaw——"

"We are not interested in your barracks gossip, sir."

"How dare you so defame him?" almost screamed Lady Gordon.

"Why, I had no wish to do that, my lady, but Prince or Pretender, he is only flesh and blood." The officer shrugged his shoulders. "Lud! we waste time. Be good enough to pack what gear you will need—and as little as possible, I pray—and accompany me without delay."

"Sir"—the colour stained Lady Ogilvy's blanched cheeks—"I beg of you—— My Lady Gordon—— 'Tis not advisable or seemly or wise for her——"

"What's amiss with her, your ladyship? She looks stout enough."

"She is—— She is with child, sir."

"Oh, that is no matter. Cannot be far gone from the look of her." The officer grinned. "And I have merely your own word for her being in that situation."

"It is true," Lady Gordon whispered.

"The Young Pretender has lost no time. He only left Glasgow in January. Eh?"

"Sir, how dare you? Oh, if my spouse were here!"

"Well, he en't. Now, I'll have no tears or vapours. You,

H

ma'am, change your fine gown, and I'd recommend the breeding lady to find a second shoe."

The two women looked helplessly at one another. Lady Ogilvy spoke clearly.

"Do you desire me to shift my attire with a gentleman in the room, sir?"

"I'll go outside. Mind! no tricks. And make haste."

He slammed the door. It shut on a clink of metal and a coarse laugh.

Lady Gordon swayed towards her friend. "Margaret! Margaret!"

"My poor Janet! But we must not stay to weep. Where is your cloak? Take this one of mine and pray that we are not separated."

"The unhappy Prince!"

"But if—if he rode away, he may effect his escape."

There was a curt knocking on the door. Lady Ogilvy opened it instantly. A man's hand thrust in Lady Gordon's missing shoe and tried to squeeze Lady Ogilvy's fingers as she took the object. With a tartan plaid over her ball-gown and Lady Gordon's finery concealed by the borrowed cloak they walked out quietly. Major Cheeseman, lounging against the wall, exchanging anecdotes of the battle with a younger officer, straightened himself and bowed awkwardly.

"A punctual woman is a rare discovery, eh, Beilby? Come along, my pretties. Ah! here is Shelmerdine with the other turtle-doves."

Under the guard of a second Whig officer Lady Kinloch and Lady Mackintosh were approaching. The four women exchanged forlornly brave smiles. Each carried her head high, disdaining to show panic or apprehension before these coarse-faced, red-coated men, but the heart of each felt like lead in her bosom. The Prince defeated, a fleeing fugitive, his army routed, his hopes fallen to dust. How cruel! How unexpected! How monstrous! And what of husbands, sons, brothers, kinsmen, mown down on that fatal field? Eyes, bright with unshed tears, asked this, whilst proud lips smiled a reassurance none felt.

"We are ready, sir," Lady Kinloch announced calmly.

Behind a file of soldiers they were marched out. It was a bitterly cold evening and Lady Gordon, sick and faint, swayed, shuddering, against her companion's shoulder. Major Cheeseman bestowed a lively curse on the climate as he stepped through the doorway, and turned to scold the prisoners for their unsuitable attire.

"Why are you dressed up like this? Ball-gowns? Powdered hair? Bah!"

"We were preparing to attend a ball, sir, to celebrate the Prince Regent's triumph." Lady Mackintosh spoke quietly.

"Oh, was you? Then let me tell you, ma'am, that his Royal Highness the Duke of Cumberland is going to lead you up to a dance you didn't expect. Ho! ho!"

The four shivered, but not with the chill of the sleety wind meeting their unprotected faces. Did the coarse jest hint at the gallows-tree?

"Margaret"—Lady Gordon clung to Lady Ogilvy's arm— "this is a just punishment for my unfilial disobedience and ingratitude, I verily believe. If I had not eloped with my spouse from my father's house this misfortune could not have chanced."

"I did not elope, but wedded with my father's consent and blessing. Nevertheless, I am here in the same plight." Lady Ogilvy pressed the cold, trembling little hand that lay near her heart. "Courage, Janet! All is not lost. We may yet foot it in St. James's."

CHAPTER XIX

RANALD CAMERON AWOKE OUT OF SLEEP. AT FIRST HE THOUGHT that he was still upon the misfortunate night-march and had roused from his slumber by the side of the road. Then, gradually and painfully, he raised his head and stared about him. It was dusk, cold and lightless, and a powdering of snow lay over everything. He saw it whitening the low park walls, the clumps of furze, the uneven ground. Where was he? In his ears there hummed a low sound of singing—a woman's milking-song—and the steady splash of milk into a pail. Was he asleep or dreaming? Peggie, she had said her name was, Peggie of the yellow hair. He thought of the sun on gorse or broom, and those soft locks were no less bright. His hand wandered out to stroke them and encountered hard earth, damp and sticky. In the failing light he saw that his fingers were stained with blood.

Reality came painfully back to him. There had been a battle. He was lying here on the plain called Drummossie, wounded, alone, perhaps forsaken by others of the clan. What of Lochiel, the Prince, the Cause? He groaned faintly. Was all lost?

There seemed to be a leaping light stabbing the dimness of air and far-off sky. Last night they had lighted bonfires to delude the enemy, but these were long since burned out. Who was feeding and tending a fire on this moor? He strained his eyes and saw that the flames were striking upwards through the roof of a rough building, probably barn or hovel. Around it figures capered and shouted. Was it his fancy or did their coats match the hue of the flames? Hanoverian soldiers! What foul work were they about?

He lay down again, but something told him that those motionless, mangled heaps all round him were dead men. The day was not too dark to see plaid or kilt clothing them. The Prince's army! He groaned, and it was as though the sound awoke an echo from the blazing barn. Human voices rose in a wild chorus of agony and appeal. Inside the building men were being roasted alive while the red-coats danced and enjoyed the spectacle.

What would be his fate when they came to where he lay? If he feigned death he might save his miserable life.

The frost soaked into his tattered clothing. He became aware of blood oozing from side and chest. He had been wounded, then.

It was growing dark. He saw forms moving about and shut his eyes. What was death but release, relief, rest? He prayed that they might strike quickly.

A figure on horseback was riding through the grey mist. From the attention and deference this man received it was obviously Cumberland himself. He halted and addressed a young officer who was lying on the ground, staring almost contemptuously at the victors. Ranald heard the harsh, guttural accents of the conqueror.

"To which party do you belong?"

The answer came clear and unhesitating. "To the Prince's."

Cumberland roared out an oath. "Shoot him!" he ordered. The officer addressed refused. Cumberland repeated his direction to a second, with the same result. Finally he turned to an ordinary soldier, barking furiously: "Shoot the dog of a rebel!" A loud explosion followed. The prone form quivered and lay still. Cumberland laughed——

The dead and wounded were stripped. Naked, the bodies

lay on the pitiless ground. Ranald Cameron feigned death. Night came, with its piercing cold and frosty stars surveying the scene of carnage and desolation from a cloudless, indifferent sky. He felt weak, inert, curiously uncaring of what would befall him. In a few hours, perchance less, he might be beyond those stars, knowing what prophets and righteous men, yea, even kings and princes, had never learned.

At intervals he saw a movement, a figure, but paid little heed. There were ghouls in women's guise who followed after a battle like buzzards scenting carrion, and stole from the dead. Here came such an one, a plaid about her slenderness. She knelt beside him and said his name.

"Ranald Cameron of Lochiel's clan?"

"Peggie? Peggie of the yellow hair?"

"Can you stand? See, take my arm, lean on me."

"What has chanced?"

"Do not heed. Be very quiet. Come!"

She was strong, for all her slightness. He hung upon her shoulder, stumbling beside her. The miles seemed endless. At times he thought that he was upon the night-march and forced himself to stand erect, to walk steadily, to advance at the head of his men. The country was wide, deserted, full of sighing winds and nameless terrors. For the last half-mile she had to drag him along, exerting all her strength. As the white walls of the farm of the Yellow Knowe glimmered out of the dark he fell, senseless. She bit her lip, lifted him, and staggered with her burden towards a barn beside the house. In the warm hay he lay motionless, and blood from his wounds stained the dry, sweet-smelling swathes.

The hours stole by. She crouched beside him, waiting until consciousness should return. The horror of the past day seemed to lurk in the shadows of the barn. Owls cried in the near-by wood. Once a mouse ran out of a hole and tore across the floor in a flurry of fear. She dared not leave him to fetch restoratives, to summon aid——

At last he stirred. She said his name, unconscious that she used it. He murmured hers.

"Where am I?"

"At my father's farm."

"But he—— You?"

"All are bedded and asleep. It is well. If the soldiers should come this way——"

"Tell me what chanced."

She shook her head in the darkness. "There was a battle. It

did not last one half-hour. Your Prince was defeated and, they say, many slain."

He groaned weakly. Was this the end of the Cause and the Stuart star a fallen one? Wearily he asked: "Where is Tearlach?"

"The Prince? I cannot tell. He rode from the field."

"And may reach safety?"

"Only God knows."

He lay panting. His wounds, which Peggie had roughly bandaged with a piece of stuff torn from her petticoat, pained him. Idly he wondered how she had come to seek him out. Was it chance, Fate, or did some unknown urge lead her to the spot where he lay on that sodden field?

"Why did you make search for me?" he murmured.

"I had to come. I could not leave you there."

The words satisfied him. He relaxed into half-sleep, part-stupor, and she knelt beside him. Once she offered to fetch food, but he shook his head feebly. He felt neither hunger nor thirst.

A thin slant of moon silvered the barn roof and sent long fingers of light through its cracks.

What was that sound? She rose from her knees and crept towards the door. Outside everything seemed utterly quiet, the dew-pearled fields, the silent wood, save for a confused noise—tramping and singing—that was steadily approaching. She stood peering into the night. A small body of men made a blot of moving darkness. Soldiers! Cumberland's red-coats! And behind, in that barn, a wounded man from the Prince's army lay, unable to effect his escape, to defend himself, to hide. She was powerless, a weak girl. If they came to the farm——

She crouched in the shadow of the barn, listening, waiting. Loud voices, mingled in dispute and contention, reached her ear, though she could discern no words. At length the noisy argument ended and she realised that the men had turned back. Oh, God be thanked! She strained her eyes, striving to make out the direction they had taken. In her absorption she did not heed another form, stealing silently out of the shadows.

"Good day," said Enoch Bradshaw.

She gazed at him, summoning her fluttering courage, her mother-wit. He did not look formidable. He had a round, high-coloured, foolish face and a shock of untidy flaxen hair.

She smiled, saying with well-simulated coquetry: "Oh, sir, how you startled me!"

He shook his head at the strange tongue. Had she no English? Peggie shook hers. "Inglissh? Na," she whispered.

He looked appraisingly at her. For a Scotchwoman she was not too ill-favoured. He liked 'em fair-haired. Reminded him of Bess.

She asked stumblingly, using the very few words of his language which she knew: "The Duke? Battle?"

"That's it, my pretty one. A great battle."

Her hands gestured eagerly. He grinned.

"You ask who won? Why, the Duke, o' course, Billy of Cumberland. God bless him, and confound all his enemies, I says."

By smile and nods she strove to convey her delight. Enoch laughed.

"You're a dainty piece of goods, my little Whig. Come with me and I'll tell you all about it."

She had no doubt as to what the invitation, emphasized by his leer, meant. In stark fear for herself, as well as for Ranald Cameron, she shrank back.

"Shy? Eh?" He was coming nearer, was almost upon her. His grin showed yellow teeth like a dog's.

Her out-thrust hands strove to fend him off.

"Come along." To her sick horror he had caught her wrist and was dragging her towards the barn.

Her free hand gestured in the direction of the wood. He turned his head, momentarily releasing her.

The other hand went to her bosom. Like all Highland girls she carried a little knife there——

Enoch Bradshaw lay very still, as still as those other forms sprawled on Culloden Moor. A look of blank surprise, of puzzled bewilderment was stamping his commonplace features. He would never see Gloucestershire again, never dally with Bess behind a haystack, never march with the other red-coats, or toast William of Cumberland. He was dead, one more victim of a Stuart Prince's frenzied ambition. Peggie of the yellow hair withdrew the knife, wiped it, replaced it, and went back to the barn.

The place was very quiet. Ranald Cameron, huddled amongst the hay, looked up as she reappeared.

"Peggie?"

"I am here. Did you think I had left you?"

"No, but I feel—strange. Stay by me."

She crouched by his side. She had seen Death before and knew that he was not a great way off.

He murmured something about the cold.

"I will wrap your plaid round you. There! Is that warmer?"

The grey lips uttered a faint negative. She gathered the slack body up in her arms. The warmth of her soft flesh made him draw a contented sigh.

"Hold me. I am dying. It is for the Prince, but—but—I do not want to die."

She cradled his head, bending her own, her breath upon his cheek.

"Has he escaped?"

"I do not know."

"If he has, I am more content to die."

"Try to sleep. I shall not leave you."

His eyes closed. Twice or thrice he whispered disjointed words or fragments of sentences. She made out Lochiel's name and once a woman's—Morag—which caused her to draw in her breath sharply. Had he a bride, a betrothed? Did another girl watch and weep for him, a girl who might never learn the fate which had overtaken him? He spoke again. "Morag! Morag!"

" 'Tis not Morag. I am only Peggie." Her voice broke on a sob.

"I thought Morag was here."

"Nay. Tell me of her."

He smiled, a contented smile like a child's.

"She is very small. I think she comes of the fairy people. Her eyes are blue—as blue as a Highland loch, and her hair is redder than yours. To me she seems beautiful."

"And you are her lover—her betrothed?"

"I love her, but I have not told her." His face grew wan and shadowed. "I shall never tell her now," he moaned.

"Tell me instead. Think that I am she."

He said again the name she was beginning to hate. "Morag! Morag!"

Her arms laid him down on the hay. A great distance seemed to divide them.

Could she have done what I have done? wondered Peggie of the yellow hair. For your sake, that that English brute-beast might not find you, I killed him. There is blood upon my hands, Ranald Cameron of Lochiel's clan.

"Lift me again," he panted.

She set her teeth and gathered his heavy body afresh in her arms.

His lips moved. She caught confused words, amongst them the name Glenfinnan. His mind was wandering through past scenes. She listened, hungry for the other woman's name——

"We gathered to march there. The standard was to be raised. Lochiel had seven hundred of us at his heels. I mind it was a very still, hot day, but the mist turned to drizzle. It aye rains in Glenfinnan. Do ye know it?"

"No." Her voice sounded harsh.

"The hills are dark and steep and the water lies at their feet. The Prince came early in a little boat. When he stepped ashore he found none to greet him, and only the bleating of sheep or the crying of whaups in the stillness. The Camerons were late. It was a long march. I can see him now, very tall, with the sun on his hair, and no pine in Lochaber stood straighter. The standard was raised and he spoke to us and we cheered him till the mountains echoed the noise. Tearlach! Tearlach!"

On the final syllable Ranald Cameron lifted himself, slid from her hold, and lay still. A woman's heart is a strange thing. As she closed his eyes she told herself that she was glad the last name upon his lips had been the Prince's, not the unknown Morag's whom he had loved.

CHAPTER XX

SIMON FRASER, THE MASTER OF LOVAT, HAD BEEN TOO LATE FOR the battle of Culloden. At the time of Charles's defeat and rout he was approaching Inverness in command of certain Frasers. The remainder of the clan who had come out were on the field with their colonel, Charles Fraser of Inverallachy. Lord Lovat's heir looked sulky and felt aggrieved. No, he decided sourly, he had not been well treated. His thoughts went back to the peaceful months at St. Andrews, his fellow-students, the congenial life there, and his resentment grew as he realized that all this was ended. Normally, on leaving the University at the completion of his studies an agreeable period of foreign travel would have lain before him, but instead—— He was ordered home abruptly the previous summer and found Castle Downie, his home, in a curious state of mingled tension, suspicion, and activity. What part was his father playing?

The young man—he was only nineteen—had all th
eighteenth-century awe of a parent, and my Lord Lovat,
stern father, was, besides, almost a legendary figure in th
neighbourhood and to all Scotland. His son distrusted certai
things which showed plainly. Why were some seven hundre
clansmen being sedulously drilled? What lay behind the pu
chase of tents and warlike equipment? There had alway
been a considerable amount of mystery in his father's life, an
Simon Fraser the younger knew that his lordship had change
sides in politics more than once, but which would he espous
now? The boy, idle, sullen, saw plenty to puzzle him.

It was a windless September morning, the wasps drows
amongst the fruit, and he himself was setting out to enjoy som
hours' fishing on the Beauly. Sulkily he had followed th
clansman who had summoned him to his father's presence
pondering how long he might be kept, whether his sport mus
be abandoned, and why he was needed. Although a spell o
excessively mild weather prevailed a huge fire burned in th
grate, and Lord Lovat, gouty, gross, unwieldy, sprawled befor
it. He seemed in an unusually good temper, chuckling anc
grinning. By his side lay a packet, newly opened, and from
it he took a paper——

"Good morning, child."

"Good morning, my lord."

"Sit down. I have some news."

The Master of Lovat subsided uneasily on a chair. His
glance wandered to the window. Beyond, spread the ripe,
smiling country, open, magnificent, colourful, but here in
this close room the sombre figures of treachery, conspiracy,
cunning, and chicanery seemed to loom. Robert Chevis of
Muirtown, who lived some two miles away and was constantly
at Castle Downie, was present, together with my lord's secretary, Robert Fraser. The wrinkled old hand held out the
paper.

"Read it!" Lord Lovat ordered his son.

"But what is it, my lord?"

"Read it!"

The boy rose, advanced unwillingly, and took the
document.

He had understood its contents and purport in a flash.
Here were Prince Charles Edward's declaration and manifesto.
He stammered as much and his father grinned afresh.

"Well, my son, show that your education has not been

wasted. Read it aloud for myself and these gentlemen to
hear."

Robert Chevis interposed sharply.

"My lord, I object. Such a document should not be read."

"Chevis, you talk treason."

"No, my lord. 'Tis not right or fitting for the young man to
read such stuff."

"Havers! Read it, I tell you, boy."

He had obeyed, stumbling a little. Lord Lovat chuckled.

"Chevis, I offer you a captain's commission in the service of
your lawful Prince."

"He is not my lawful Prince, my lord."

"He is mine. I am to join the Prince's party and to live and
die in that Cause. Why, man, success is sure, as sure as God is
in heaven."

He had left them quarrelling and stumbled out of the room.
Chevis had stalked from the house and discontinued his visits,
but Robert Fraser, the dark-faced secretary, knew much——

Lord Lovat was grumbling at the rising of the Highlands.
He had always considered Lochiel a man of sense and prudence, yet he had brought out his clan. Cluny, his lordship's
son-in-law, was equally rash. The MacDonalds were all out,
and on every side there was rumour of the Prince's growing
success. Which way would the cat jump?

There were many letters to Duncan Forbes of Culloden,
Lord President of the Court of Session, Lord Lovat's crony,
and—as distances went in the country—his neighbour. Forbes
was no fool. He knew—he must know—that Castle Downie
was playing a double game. The Prince wanted Lord Lovat,
less as combatant than as adviser and follower, and if the
Frasers came out, others would rise. The bait offered was
mighty tempting. James III and VIII would offer rich reward
to those who supported his son, when that son, or himself, sat
in St. James's. Lord Lovat, wary and waiting, demanded an
earnest of favours to come. Let the Prince make him Duke of
Beaufort and he would serve him. A messenger was sent
to Charles at Invergarry, outlining Lord Lovat's proposed
plans, and the young man grinned when he recalled Fraser
of Gortuleg's return, without the patent, and the information
that, disregarding Lord Lovat's advice, the Prince was marching southward into the Atholl country instead of coming
north through Stratherrick as his lordship had counselled.
How angry his father's voice sounded as he stormed at the

unlucky doer. Even the heavy door and thick walls failed to shut out the sounds——

And then—— And then—— Simon Fraser marched in front of his men, shrugging his shoulders at the cold, and recalled the weeks which followed. The Prince, in his father's phrase, bade fair to be master of Scotland. Perth, Edinburgh, the Lowlands were all his. At Holyrood more of the clans came in, and news trickled north of an invasion of England. He did not know even now how it had fallen out, but the Highland army was back in Scotland, and half-way through a December of biting frost and dour rains the blow fell.

He was ordered to march with certain of the Frasers to join the Prince. It was the safest game to play, for the father to stay at home, the son to go out. Thus necks and estates were saved in the event of failure. He had sulked and refused —as far as he dared. He knew that his father was fooling Forbes of Culloden and had gone so far as to put the blame for the Frasers' defection on his son. What imbecility! Lord Lovat reigned as absolute king over the clan and without his orders or permission not a single clansman, much less his heir, would have dared to stir a finger. His cheek burned as he remembered the scene which preceded his departure, an accidental sight of a letter describing him as stiff-necked and disobedient, his wild threats to disclose all to the Lord President, and his childish rage in which he hurled his bonnet, ornamented with a white cockade, into the fire. Nothing had availed him. In command of some hundred Frasers he marched these, through bleak, wild country, to Fort Augustus, where a kind of blockade was formed. It was a feeble, futile attempt to reduce the fortress. The frost was cruel, the men's hearts hardly in the business, he himself untrained, ignorant of the art of war, thrust into a position of authority for which he had no liking. Small wonder that when Lord Loudoun, with six hundred of the well-affected clans, marched from Inverness through Stratherrick, part of Lord Lovat's estate—what irony! —he met with no opposition. The Frasers retired to Perth and into the Lowlands to Stirling. The Prince was besieging Stirling Castle. Young, impressionable, trying to hate him, the boy was brought into his presence at Bannockburn House——

He did not know what he had expected to see. Charles was past the first glow of enthusiasm and success, but he was still good to look upon, regal, royal, and gracious. Simon Fraser kissed his hand. So my Lord Lovat had moved at last? the Prince asked.

"I am here in his stead, sir."

"But he designs to come, to join me?" The high voice was eager.

"I do not know, sir. My father is an old man. The fatigues of a campaign——" The boy stammered and hesitated.

"Nonsense!" cried the Prince. "Every care would be taken of him. My Lord Pitsligo, who is of an advanced age, has withstood the hardships of my expedition to England and back without harm."

The boy dropped his eyes. He felt ashamed and uneasy.

Charles questioned him avidly as to the position of affairs in the north. The Duke of Gordon had refused to come out, but Lord Lewis Gordon, despite difficulties, had collected many men from Aberdeenshire. Was that not so? MacDonald of Barrisdale, young Glengarry, and the elder Lochiel had brought reinforcements from the west. Glengyle was in command of certain MacGregors from Perthshire. As for the ladies—— The Prince laughed with some embarrassment. Lady Mackintosh had raised her clan under MacGillvray of Dunmaglass, although her husband was with the Government, and Lady Fortrose, whose spouse was with Lord Loudoun, had sent Charles some Mackenzies. Lord Cromarty had joined, with a Mackenzie regiment. Was the Master of Lovat acquainted with his son, Lord MacLeod? *Comment?* They were of an age and friends. *Bon! bon!*

He had been graciously dismissed, half under the spell of the Prince's vivid personality and captivating charm which swayed so many——

Falkirk! It was whispered that the Prince had won his last success. He remembered wind and rain, the mad chase after Hawley's flagging troops, the confusion and argument and recriminations following, young Glengarry's untimely fate, the crazy decision to continue with the siege of Stirling Castle. The Master of Lovat hunched his shoulders. It was all madness. To have landed at all was an act of crass folly, but to come without assistance, or the promise of any foreign aid, spelled ruin from the start.

He had sat with the chiefs whilst they debated a further retreat to the north. His signature was added to those of the rest when a formal petition had been drawn up, requesting the Prince to consent to retire to the Highlands. The result was only what might have been anticipated. Charles had flown into a passion, argued, appealed, refused, finally capitulated, amid bitter reproaches. The actual retreat was confusion, muddle, neglect, and almost disaster. Lord George Murray blamed O'Sullivan. The Prince haughtily shouldered the responsibility. How could the Cause ever prosper with the leaders for ever at variance, the Prince too ready to be swayed by flatterers and foreigners? And now—— The end?

The stripling sent a sulky order to his men to halt and stared about him. They were just outside Inverness and it seemed to him that the usual sleepy indifference of the town was stirred by some untoward excitement. Men stood round in small groups, heads nodding, lips thrust out, a general air as of an event of importance being under discussion. The atmosphere was very still, but through the heavy haze which overhung everything a muffled noise like that of guns firing at a distance smote on the ear. He frowned. Guns? That meant fighting. Was the Prince at last fronting Cumberland? Had he the smallest chance of success?

He went aside and accosted a gentleman with whom he had some slight acquaintance. "Pray, sir, enlighten me. There seems some stir toward."

"I regret that I can tell you little, sir." The answer came stiffly. "I understand that the Duke of Cumberland's forces have engaged those of the Young Pretender."

The Master of Lovat bit his lip. A dour loyalty towards his father led him to correct the speaker. "Shall we say the Chevalier, sir?"

"Your pardon, sir. I had overlooked that you was on the Jacobite side."

"Which is, I trust, the victorious one?"

The other hesitated. "I am not in a position to inform you. There has been a battle, I understood."

"'Has been'? Is it, then, over?"

"I was told so."

The young man stood irresolute. His acquaintance moved away with a brief bow. What was the truth? The stir around him was increasing. He caught passing words, brief references to the "the Pretender," "the Duke," "a rousing defeat," and similar vague and non-committal phrases, but nothing conclusive or certain. As he waited, chafing with impatience, undecided, apprehensive, two gentlemen on horseback approached. One was Mr. Baillie of Aberichan, the other Mr. Maxwell of Morphy. He knew both. Lord Lovat had sneered

requently at the lukewarm Jacobitism of Aberichan. Quickly
he stepped forward, arresting their passage.

"Sir, I beg of you—— What news?"

"News, sir?" Mr. Baillie seemed heated and angry. "I
have none to give you."

"Has there not been a battle? I was informed——"

"And what right had you to loiter here, awaiting tidings?
Why were you not with your Prince?"

"Caution, Aberichan," murmured Mr. Maxwell.

"Caution? Caution? Do not use that word to me, I beg,
sir. I regret extremely that I yielded to your solicitations to
accompany you this day. A more grievous spectacle I could
not wish to behold."

Mr. Baillie's raised, heated accents were attracting the attention of loiterers and starers. His friend laid a warning hand
upon his arm. It was angrily shaken off.

"I will not be silent, sir. You invited me to witness a battle.
A more sore butchery was never seen."

"Tush! the fortunes of war."

"War, sir, but not the cold-blooded slaughter of unarmed
men. Did you not perceive that the vengeance of the military
was being wreaked on the hapless peasantry who were merely
near the spot as spectators?"

"Battles are not fought without the innocent being
involved."

"A bloody, brutal business! I can scarce credit that it
had the Duke's countenance."

"The victor of Culloden," intoned Mr. Maxwell solemnly.

"A mighty cheap victory. The enemy were half-starved,
ill-equipped, with no stomach for fighting. Pah! Victory!"

The Master of Lovat spoke through dry lips. "Is the Prince
defeated, sir?"

Mr. Baillie answered by a grim nod.

"Where is he?"

"I do not know. When the ranks broke he turned his
horse's head and rode away."

"Surely not of his own free will?"

"He may have been forced off the field." Mr. Baillie
frowned. "The smoke and the mist were very thick. They
confused objects at a distance. I was unable to discern precisely
what occurred, but I saw him riding from the scene."

"Alone?"

"I have already stated that I could see nothing very clearly.
He may have been persuaded by his friends to retreat as

speedily as possible. We did not remain to watch his motions
Our own position, with stray bullets flying everywhere, wa
vastly disagreeable."

The Master of Lovat retorted sharply: "Why was you there
sir?"

Mr. Baillie of Aberichan looked slightly abashed. To thi
stripling of nineteen he did not care to admit that he had
been lured to Drummossie through the unwise entreaties of
Mr. Maxwell of Morphy, stimulated by his own reprehensible
curiosity. He said stiffly:

"My friend Mr. Maxwell called upon me with word that
a battle was impending. He proposed that we should ride to
view the scene. We found ourselves regrettably close to the
operations. I judged it best to retire as speedily as was com-
patible with dignity, particularly when the Duke of Cumberland's men appeared to be out of hand."

"And the Prince has fled—defeated?"

"He had no chance from the first. It was all over in less
than forty minutes."

"Could not a stand have been made?"

"Impossible! In addition to the deficiencies already
enumerated he lacked half his forces."

"But can nothing be done, sir? The bridge? Could we not
defend its passage? If we were to fight here——"

Mr. Baillie lost his temper. As well as realizing that he had
displayed an unbecoming and cold-blooded curiosity, levelling
himself to the rank of common fellows like his blacksmith, he
had had a narrow escape of being hit, and possibly killed. Fear
often leads to anger. He unleashed his wrath on the nearest
possible object. Who was this boy, who should have had his
men on the field to lend their aid, that he was now anxious
to use his sword an hour too late? Irritably Mr. Baillie
retorted:

"Fighting! By ——, Master, you were not in the way
when fighting might have been of service. You had better
now say nothing about it."

The young man flushed furiously. The rebuke was, in a
measure, just, but ought rather to have been addressed to the
wary, crafty old man fourteen miles away at Gortuleg, antici-
pating a Jacobite victory and ordering savoury meats to be
prepared to celebrate the same.

CHAPTER XXI

APRIL OF THAT FATED YEAR—1746—WAS A DOUR MONTH. THE cold bit like a newly-whetted dirk and the snow seemed as though no sun would ever melt it. Day after day Lord Lovat shivered over the fire at Gortuleg House. It was a plain, white-harled, long building, with little windows that looked across fields where a few patches of green showed amongst muddy slush, and the mountains reared against a sullen sky.

On the sixteenth of April, Gortuleg had been a hive of industry since early morning. Men, wearing the Fraser tartan, hurried in and out. In the kitchen a mighty smell of cooking testified to preparations for a great feast. The Prince's victory, Lord Lovat declared, must be celebrated fittingly. Since his arrest by Lord Loudoun the previous December and his canny escape from Inverness he had lived at Gortuleg very privately, but a corps of swift-footed young clansmen brought him intelligence of all that was going on. He felt confident and easy in his mind. That lawyer-body, Duncan Forbes, had had to depart in undignified haste for Skye, and Prince Charles's troops were drinking his good wine stored at Culloden House. An auld wifie, Duncan, with his lang neb and his dislike of tea. They said that in Edinburgh to encourage people to take less tea he drank whisky. Well, well, folks must have their foibles. He had seen enough of life to realize that it took all sorts to make a world.

At intervals he heaved himself out of his great chair and hobbled, groaning and grunting, to the kitchen. The cook, stirring or basting or wielding a mighty rolling-pin, would look up from her task to see the gross old face and leering eyes keeking in at the door. She shook the rolling-pin at him and he paid her compliments in Gaelic and inquired how her cooking sped. With a shrug of her ample shoulders she vowed that if she were left in peace her preparations would go forward more smoothly and speedily. Lord Lovat ambled in and squeezed her comely bulk. She gave him a rap with the wooden pin and he let out a skirl which brought half the household running, my lord's secretary amongst them. Lord Lovat declared that she had broken his head and his death would lie at her door, and there was wailing and reproaches, in the midst of which Grizel Fraser returned to her cooking. It was no use paying any attention to the chief. He liked his jest and knew

I

how far he might go with her, but she preferred her kitchen to herself.

Lord Lovat lumbered back to the fire. Although he had weathered Scots springs in plenty his aged bones felt the cold. He screeched at one of his clansmen to pile on logs, and stretched his swollen old limbs towards the leaping heat. The wind had wailed all day, a low, pitiful keening, the door-snecks rattled and the chimneys smoked. No definite news had arrived. Crofter or tacksman crept at intervals to the door, but these brought little save rumour or surmise. My lord was tortured with gout and his temper such that his secretary took good care to keep out of reach of the great stick propped beside his chair. To divert his chief's mind he drew him back to old days and asked him of his adventures.

"Ay, I was younger then," he growled.

"But you had foes, my lord," Robert Fraser reminded him.

"Ay, had I," he muttered. "That daft-like marriage of mine to the Dowager Lady Lovat brought the whole clam-jamphry of the Murrays about my ears like a nest of hornets." He rumbled with laughter. "They're a' in this ploy now, Duke William and his brother Lord George, and the daft pack of 'em, saving the Duke of Atholl himself. James is a wise man. He's not going to risk his neck for a jack o' lantern."

The secretary concluded from this that my lord had no great opinion of the Atholl Murrays, excepting Lord George. The latter, Lord Lovat was wont to declare, was the only soldier in the Prince's army. The rest were hot-heads, in-capables, whilst as for Secretary Murray——

"'Tis over forty years syne," he went on. He huddled nearer to the peats, a vast hulk of a man, shapeless and obese, yet with the remains of dignity and grandeur about him. "Go and see if the door be shut. There's a cursed draught some-where."

Robert Fraser shook the door and felt the wind seeping in beneath. A rattle of sleet against the windows followed and my lord heaped objurgations on the cold, saying old blood ran thin.

"Seventeen hundred and two," he mumbled. "Ay, the year I went to France."

The secretary licked his lips, for he knew from old talk that Lord Lovat had had his finger in a fine pie at that time. King William was dead, and France and England fighting just as they were in 1744. There were plums for the picking. King James's widow, Queen Mary, she who had been Mary

Beatrice of Modena, kept the hope of the throne of England before her son, but a child then, and held court at St. Germain, surrounded mostly by needy adherents, futile plotters, and quarrelling time-servers. A man required a steady head to steer his path between these and hold his own advantage.

If anybody could it was my Lord Lovat. The secretary said something of the kind and he looked up with his wolf's grin.

"Right, Robert Fraser, ay, very right. I had little to thank Scotland for. Was I not outlawed, and intercommuned at Inverness Cross? 'Twas said I had forfeited my rights to the Lovat estates. Letters of fire and sword went out against me. Oh! I ken fine what you would say. The King pardoned me and absolved me of treason, but not of a worse charge. I had the Murrays ever at my heels and even Argyll, my friend once, turned his face from me. It was but wisdom to see how matters went in France."

"And the Queen, my lord? Your lordship saw her?"

"Och, ay! A plain woman, ye ken, with a tricky skein to unravel. She was living on King Louis's bounty and it would never do to offend him. Na, na. And she trusted my Lord Middleton and the Duke of Perth though it was the clash of Paris that neither could thole the other, and they were the chief men about her court. A man had to take sides—Middleton or Perth."

"And you, my lord?"

"Perth was my choice, man, and Middleton ne'er forgave me for it. Weel, they're both dead, and the world not much better or much worse for either of them. What's that ye say? Speak louder. I doubt I'm growing deaf."

The secretary knew well that Lord Lovat was not, but he had a trick of pretending not to hear and thus leading others on to speak incautiously. Robert Fraser replied that he was asking whether my lord saw the French king.

"O' course I did. He was mighty civil to a Highland chief and a young man of promise. I was that then, but it's all by wi' and come to naught—naught." He sat brooding.

"Was your lordship granted a private audience?"

"By the King? Ay. I had spent days and nights composing an address for the edification of His Most Christian Majesty, but at the sight of him and the splendours of the court and the clash of tongues, French and English, it gaed clean oot o' my heid."

"Vastly awkward, my lord."

"Ay, to an ordinary man, but I have gifts and parts and

my wits did not desert me altogether. I made a speech then
and there and learned afterwards that the King was well
enough pleased. Ay. Ay. The long and short o' it is the King
gave me a commission as brigadier-general, and I spent a
mighty pleasant year in France."

He grinned again and chuckled to himself.

"And then, my lord?"

"They sent me back to Scotland to test her pulse in a
manner o' speaking. I was to visit the Highlands and see
whether the times were ripe for a rising."

"The Queen sent you?"

"She gave me her countenance, but she was a puir scared
body. I must not attempt to foment a rising, but the Queen
did not know the Highlands. It was all in King Louis's favour
if they rebelled, and Louis had more to offer than a woman in
exile. Women are all weather-cocks. At first she was so
ravished with my proposals for a rising that she offered to
pledge or sell her jewels."

Lord Lovat sat chuckling and the secretary grinned to
himself. Well he knew how the conspiracy had failed for all
my lord's turning and twisting, crossing and double-crossing,
hoodwinking great nobles such as the Duke of Queensberry,
and slipping about the Highlands as supple as an eel. He asked
Lord Lovat of his journey from France.

"Oh, ay. Well, we started for Calais, where we kicked our
heels for near a month. Who were 'we,' ye'd ask? Jonie Moray,
as they called him, Captain John Murray, brother-german
to the Laird of Abercairney, was chief amongst us. King Louis
was for sending a Frenchman, but I'd take a Scot or none at
all. And was he not a subject of France? Then there were
Colonel Graham and Major George Fraser, and your humble
servant. Count de la Tour, the governor of Calais, was a canny
chiel. He gave a heavy bribe to the captain of an English
packet and he took us aboard her as prisoners of war. I mind
it was murk-dark when we landed near Dover, and had to
make our way to London. It was all mighty expensive. Oh,
I had my pension from St. Germain, and before I left France
I received five hundred *louis d'or*, but, losh! that soon melted
like snow on a dyke once the sun's keeking out.

"I bided no lang time in London, just sufficient to find
how the land lay with honest men there. The Duke of Hamilton, whom I had thought hand-in-glove with St. Germain,
would not hazard a sou for the Cause. I had good reason to
distrust Sir John MacLean, who kept nothing from his wife,

and she told secrets to her father and these went into the ear of the Government. It was mid-June when Jonie and I pushed on to Durham, expecting fresh horses and a sum of money from Scotland. We halted at a post-house at Northallerton, ourselves and our three servants. I had Tom Fraser, a gentleman of my clan, and a French valet, and many a time I rued the day I brought the rogue with me out of France. He could dress a wig to perfection, but his head was weak and when he was at the wine his tongue wagged."

"A sad failing, my lord," murmured Robert Fraser.

"It was so that night. He got to talking too freely and word stole to a pestilential justice of the peace. Jonie and I were sitting over our glass when in comes Tom Fraser, all trembling, to tell us the house was surrounded by constables. Ay, a bonnie kettle of fish."

"What did your lordship do?"

"Oh, at first I was for cutting my way through or perishing in the attempt, but Jonie Murray was no' for the risk. He was a naturalized Frenchman and that protected him. Then I armed the servants with pistols, even that French scamp who was sober enough by then and weeping for the mischief his loose tongue had set afoot. I had my own pistol cocked and was ready for the worst, when Simon Fraser began to think that in a contest of wits he might easily score over an English justice. Why should I not pretend to be brother-german to the Duke of Argyll, John Campbell of Mamore, myself travelling under my old name of Captain John Campbell?" He winked cunningly. "I had accompanied the Duke to the Northallerton races once upon a time, and could play my part with ease.

"In came the justice of the peace, a pursy little man, with a mighty good opinion of himself. I gave him no time to ask me questions, but told him how happy I was to meet him, and that it was almost two years syne I had had that pleasure with the Duke of Argyll at the races near the town. Man! he swallowed it like a Beauly salmon opening his jaws for a bait. He was all apologies to 'his lordship' for intruding, and would I honour him by cracking a bottle of wine with him. I was nothing loath, so off he sent the constables, a flea in their lugs, and a bottle of the best Spanish wine was dispatched to my room. This was only the first of a good number and the better part of them travelled down the justice's throat. In the end he had to be carried home, and we all thought it wiser not to wait till he was sober next day. It was one in the

morning when we left Northallerton, and raining just as it
has done this whole month. Now I'll take a nap and tell you the
rest another time."

CHAPTER XXII

"AUNT GRIZEL, I WANT A PIECE."
The request came from the cook's niece, Isobel Fraser,
to her overworked and harassed relative. Exasperated, Grizel
took the child of ten by the arm and thrust her into a little
closet.

"Bide ye there, bairn. Ye'll get nae piece ava till I'm
through wi' my cooking. Between ye and the chief a body has
sma' chance o' gettin' forward wi' her work."

Isobel, accustomed to be hustled and disregarded, sat down
philosophically in her temporary prison. The closet had a tiny
window which framed a portion of country below and a distant marsh, reputed to be a haunt of fairies. She gazed at this,
wondering whether the superstition were true. How wonderful
to see a fairy! It might give her a wish. What should that be?
She wanted a new tartan ribbon, and a piece of money to
spend the next time her aunt took her into Inverness, and
a gift for Mrs. Grant of Laggan who was kind to her. Perhaps
a fairy would allow her to choose one of these?

How quiet all had grown suddenly! The noise and bustle
which had awakened echoes about the old house all day had
changed to a deep silence. She grew weary of her captivity
and stole to the door. Aunt Grizel had not locked her in.
Isobel slipped out and reconnoitred. Nobody was visible
except my Lord Lovat, sunk in a deep chair, either asleep
or brooding. He paid no heed as she passed him, though
sometimes he called her to his side, pulled her hair, pinched
her pink cheek, and told her to be a good wee lass. She
pattered to the door. Outside, a smoky sunset was smeared
behind the bare tree-tops and everything looked misty, still,
featureless. The household, men and women, were grouped
together, staring towards some moving object in a declivity
below the house. Were those fairies? Isobel's little chest
heaved. Would they come nearer? She had been told—and
believed it implicitly—that fairies only remained visible to
mortals between one blink of the eyelids and the next.
Feverishly she strove to keep her eyes from closing so that the

tantalizing vision might not vanish. In spite of her efforts
the aching, rigid lids fell, but the moment she raised them
again she saw that what she had mistaken for fairies were
merely ordinary human beings. A body of horsemen was
approaching. They seemed to surround, nay, to guard, a tall,
fair-haired young man, who looked strangely dishevelled and
distraught. He swung down from his mount, and in a few
minutes a tumult of sounds filled the air, women's cries, loud
objurgations in Gaelic, lamentations and curses. The child
stared, bewildered. Who were these?

She was not long left in doubt. All Scotland had whispered
of Prince Tearlach, who had landed with an empty kist and
seven swords and naught but promises to pay for a rising, yet
had won half the country to his standard. Here he stood, but
even Isobel Fraser's girlish eyes discerned no victor, no uncrowned king. Defeat, ay, despair were written on his lined
young face and in the droop of the slender figure in its travel-
stained garments. He spoke in a highly pitched, almost
hysterical key, demanding Lord Lovat.

"Eh? Eh? Who's there? Who wants me?" inquired the
cracked accents of the Fraser chief. "Come away, gentlemen.
You will belike bring me word of a battle and the Duke's
defeat. Eh?"

"I bring you word of a defeat, my lord." The fair-haired
young man laughed terribly.

"Whose, sir, whose?"

"The Prince's."

"God save us! Who are ye?"

"Charles Edward Stuart, my lord, your rightful Prince."

"Come your ways in," muttered my Lord Lovat.

They went into the house, the girl stealing after, fearful,
yet her small being thrilling with curiosity. Was this indeed
Tearlach in the flesh?

The two were face to face, the gross old man, with his
swollen body, crafty brain, and imperilled future, and the
young Prince who had seen his hopes, his crown, his dreams
destroyed before his eyes. They embraced, French fashion, and
Charles said hoarsely: "My lord, my lord, if you had been
with us, perchance this might not have fallen out."

Lord Lovat's shifty gaze could not meet the Prince's haggard eyes. He mumbled excuses in English, excuses noted by
the greedy ears of Robert Fraser who had pressed into the
room with others.

"I was unable, to my deep regret, to join your Royal Highness in person. My age—— My health—— I did all I could, sir, upon my honour."

"Mighty little, my lord." The Prince's lip curled.

"Was it little, sir, to have sent my son Simon, my heir, whom I love more than myself, to serve you?"

"You yourself would have been of greater importance, my Lord Lovat. Your zeal, your presence must have induced others to espouse my Cause."

"I sent my clan. I sent my clan," Lord Lovat almost screamed.

"But a handful. And even most of those were not present at to-day's ruffle, my lord."

Lord Lovat gestured angrily, glanced about him, saw that his secretary was obviously listening, and broke abruptly into French, a language with which Robert Fraser was not acquainted.

"One defeat does not mean irrevocable loss, sir."

"To me it does, my lord."

"Then what, may I ask, does your Royal Highness design to do?"

Charles had sunk into a chair, the image of misery and dejection. He did not raise his head as he replied.

"I can see nothing for it save to return to France."

The word, the suggestion sent the hoary old chief into a paroxysm of fury.

"To France? Your Royal Highness proposes to abandon your army, your friends, your Cause, Scotland itself, and retreat to the Continent? Bah!"

"What other can I attempt? My army is defeated, many slain, the remainder fleeting for their lives. My friends are proscribed, fugitive; Scotland at the mercy of the Duke of Cumberland. In France I can plead my need in person to King Louis. He must, he shall, aid me!"

"I thought"—Lord Lovat's gross mouth sneered—"that when your Royal Highness landed you swore that you would skulk amongst the mountains with six stout, trusty fellows rather than go back to France."

The Prince's shaking hands covered his face.

"Is it the act of a friend, my lord, to taunt those fallen from high estate?"

"I do not taunt you, sir, but I never thought to see my King's son leaving Scotland to pay the piper after he had called the tune."

The Prince's tears began to fall quietly.

"How can I stay? Where could I go?" A momentary flash of spirit made him lift his chin and ask clearly: "Would you give me shelter?"

"I, sir? Impossible! My head's as much in danger as your Royal Highness's."

"Then you see, my lord. I have no friends here."

"Friends? What of the clans, sir, the loyal clans? They would gather, did you but summon them."

Charles shook a listless head.

"I do not think enough of the leaders are left to rally sufficient of their men. And how could word be sent to them—or where?"

"Did your Royal Highness appoint no place of meeting in the event of a defeat?"

"No." A hot patch of crimson suddenly dyed either hollowed cheek. "I did not think it needful."

"The mair fule, ye," muttered Lord Lovat. French and Gaelic failing him, he relapsed afresh into English. "Sir, remember your great ancestor, I beseech you, Robert the Bruce, who lost eleven battles and won Scotland by the twelfth. If I could get down on my knees I would not rise from them till I had your promise to stay and lead your Highlanders again."

"I cannot." Charles's tone was sullen. "I must reach France with all speed. 'Tis madness to linger."

"At least eat and drink, sir."

"I cannot eat. Bring me a glass of wine. That will suffice."

Lord Lovat shouted angry orders. The wine was brought. Whilst awaiting it the Prince stood about restlessly, biting his lip, glancing round him, ears alert as a hare's for treachery or danger. He took the glass in a shaking hand and drank the contents at a gulp. It was filled and refilled. His tears, the awed child noted, ran down, mingling with the wine. Then he rose again, embraced Lord Lovat a second time, his disordered fair hair falling over the other's plaid, and stumbled towards the door. My lord hobbled after him to see him and the handful he had brought with him ride away. Outside, it was very quiet, save for a woman's wailing. The sky had cleared and was a deep, dark blue, with pine trunks etched against it. Evening was coming fast. The strange, still day, which had seen the heart of Scotland broken, drew towards dusk and night. A tiny bird piped a sleepy note. Charles stared about him, at the mighty mountain-peaks, serried, indifferent, their domes still thatched in places with snow, the wild country, the shadows of woods still far from boasting their spring green. He muttered sombrely: " 'Tis a cold land." The girl, Isobel Fraser, pressed amongst the others, watched him mount, gallop forward, followed by his few adherents, and disappear into the dark. Ever afterwards she recalled little things: the tilt of his chin, the long fingers clutching a sodden bonnet, the way the firelight turned his fair hair to bronze, and the last gesture as he twisted in his saddle to wave farewell. She rubbed her eyes. Was it all a dream? Had she seen some fairy being, or was this indeed the fairy-tale Prince, Tearlach, a creature of flesh and blood? She retained a vivid impression of the scene, the incident, which never left her when she was an old woman.

The hall was full of Frasers, bawling and cursing, some weeping, some speiring for the Master of Lovat, or wailing that son or kinsman was fallen at Culloden. Lord Lovat shouted them down, overaweing them by his own passion and panic. He heaped objurgations on the Prince's head, calling him coward, faint-heart, recreant. Was he, for one defeat, to cry all lost? Nothing mattered to him, it appeared, save his own safety, his own neck. What of those whom he had ruined? Lord Lovat had staked everything, including his head. He must hide until better times.

"Robert, I'm best away."

"But where, my lord? Besides, you cannot ride."

Lord Lovat cursed his secretary and yelled orders that were confusedly obeyed. A certain amount of hurried packing, a meal devoured in hot haste, and a litter was brought to the door. Hefty clansmen heaved the groaning bundle of tartans which was the chief of the Frasers into the uncomfortable conveyance. Isobel watched the departure from behind the shelter of her Aunt Grizel's ample skirts. It was the last time many were to see Simon Fraser.

CHAPTER XXIII

MURRAY OF BROUGHTON HEARD TIDINGS OF CULLODEN ON HIS sick-bed. As he had been in a high fever it was deemed wise by those who had access to him to conceal as long as possible how complete and overwhelming the Prince's defeat must be considered. Long-faced visitors came in, took snuff, and spoke with amiable and misleading vagueness of Charles's motions. Ay, his Royal Highness, not being joined by the detached parties from his army, had retired across the Nairn to stronger ground where the enemy's horse would be useless. Murray grinned with feeble satisfaction. Before leaving Inverness he had sent repeated messages to Charles, imploring him not to risk a battle until his forces should be complete. The Prince had followed his advice. This gave him great satisfaction. On the far side of the river his Royal Highness could fight upon his own terms.

It was a trifle disturbing to the secretary next morning to have his friends come to him with a tentative suggestion that he should be conveyed across the lake to a house occupied by Grant of Glenmoriston. Mrs. Grant, he was assured, would make him welcome. Weak, reduced by fever, listless and devitalized, Mr. Murray did not inquire too particularly the reason for this solicitude and invitation. The Prince's army was entire, he concluded. The journey exhausted him still further. Mrs. Grant, fussy, excitable, received him cordially and insisted on his being carried at once to bed. The day was cold and springless, like its predecessor. He lay, half-awake, listening to the country sounds outside his window: the shrill singing of a dairy-maid over her milk pails, the pipe of birds, the wind in the bare branches. It was late afternoon before Mrs. Grant scratched on the door and put a head in a mob-cap cautiously round the opening. Would Mr. Murray feel inclined to receive a visitor?

"Why, ma'am, the gentleman would be very acceptable. I weary lying abed and hearing nothing."

"Then I shall bring him upstairs, sir?"

"Pray, ma'am, who is he? Does he come from the Prince?"

"I—I could not say, sir. 'Tis good Dr. Cameron."

"What! Lochiel's brother? None could be more welcome. Do not give yourself the trouble, though, of mounting the stairs again, ma'am, I beg. Request the doctor to enter."

Dr. Cameron appeared on the heels of the summons. Murray of Broughton raised himself in bed and expressed his pleasure at seeing him. "Pray be seated, sir. You will think me a sad lie-a-bed, but positively I am so weak that it tires me to lift my hand."

"You look a sick man," muttered Dr. Cameron.

"Ay, so I am. But for my sickness nothing would have induced me to leave the Prince and place my duties in the hands of Mr. Hay."

"Hay is a poor substitute, sir."

"I regret to hear it."

There was a long silence in the pleasant bedchamber.

"What news have you of the Prince, Dr. Cameron?"

"Very grievous news, sir."

"Grievous?"

"The most grievous possible. In your state of health I would gladly have spared you knowing of it——"

"Sir, I entreat you, tell me all. Keep nothing back. Is the Prince well?"

"His Royal Highness is well in body, but he has met with irreparable disaster."

"Of what nature?"

"Yesterday, I regret to say against the wishes of his advisers, he engaged the forces of the Duke of Cumberland. Within forty minutes his army was driven back, the clans scattered, and the Prince himself——"

"Not slain or captured? Sir, this is terrible. A moment ago you spoke of him as well in body."

"He left the field with certain of his friends. I understand he was making for Gortuleg to apprise Lord Lovat of the disastrous turn his fortunes had taken, but after that—— I do not know aught of his motions."

Mr. Murray stared in dismay at the speaker.

"But surely, sir, some place was appointed as a rendezvous in case of—of a reverse?"

"I have learned of none. The Prince, it appears, could not contemplate defeat, or the necessity of providing a rendezvous in such an event."

The sick man frowned deeply.

"What of the chiefs? Lochiel? Lord George Murray? The Duke of Perth?"

"My brother was badly wounded in both ankles with grape-shot. He must have fallen a prey to the Hanoverians' savagery had not his clansmen carried him from the field. Lord George, I understand, was unharmed, likewise His Grace of Perth."

"I implore you, sir, to say that this is but a temporary set-back. The Prince will rally the clans again. He can make a stand either at Fort Augustus or Ruthven, to prevent the enemy's advance for some time, or on the high ground keep upon the defensive the whole summer."

"I can give you no information as to his Royal Highness's intentions, sir."

Again that odd silence fell. A fly, aroused out of its winter sleep, crawled feebly up and down the window-pane in a square of pallid sunshine.

"Have you considered your own situation, Mr. Murray?" Dr. Cameron asked.

"No, sir. This intelligence leaves me no thought for other than the Prince's position. You would hint"—he smiled wryly—"that I am in danger?"

"The Duke of Cumberland has possession of Inverness. It is not improbable that parties will follow the numbers who fled from the field of battle. If I may advise, sir, I think it might be desirable for you to remove higher up the glen."

Mr. Murray gave a reluctant consent. More journeys, uncertainty, fatigues. His mouth shut sourly. It was not an inviting prospect. That evening he was again transported some miles in a litter, and by slow stages reached Fort Augustus. At Lochgarry's house he came across one Warren, who had acted as aide-de-camp to the Duke of Perth.

"This is a black business, Mr. Murray," Warren told the secretary.

"But all cannot be lost, sir. If, as I understand, no rendezvous was appointed in case of defeat, surely the clans can be gathered afresh?"

"I fear not, sir." Mr. Warren pursed up his lips. "Near to three thousand men, including the MacPhersons who were not in the action, have been dispersed."

"By whose orders, sir?"

"I understand by those of the Duke of Perth and my Lord George Murray."

Lord George's namesake looked thoughtful.

"Have you any word of His Grace, sir?"

"He is, I believe, to be this night at Invergarry. Everyone is doing the best he can for his own safety."

The secretary, worried and fretful, desired Mr. Warren to arrange a meeting with the Duke of Perth. This took place in a secluded wood some two miles from Invergarry's frowning walls. Both men were, Mr. Murray reflected grimly, in a mighty poor case. He himself had newly risen from a sick-bed and the Duke, of a weakly constitution at the best of times, was so worn out with fatigue that he appeared almost on the verge of collapse. There was, he averred wearily, no possibility of retrieving their affairs. No one seemed to know where the Prince was. Most of the chiefs were scattered and missing. Sullenly Mr. Murray agreed to continue his journey to

Lochiel's country and there await some account of Charles's
motions.

It was still cold and winterly, the road in many places deep
in snow. A rumour met him in clachan and village that Lochiel
was dead, but ultimately it transpired that he lived and had
reached his house of Achnacarry. A little later, with Stuart
of Ardshiel and some others, he joined the secretary, all broken,
proscribed men, one sick, one lamed by grape-shot, but each alike
determined to tend to a fresh blaze the flame which had set the
heather a-lowe and was all but quenched at Culloden. They
led a fugitive, hunted life, slipping from place to place, until
at length they crossed Loch Arkaig and found refuge in some
little huts which they erected in a wood. The weather was
fitful, days of spring sunshine alternating with storms of
smiting rain and the keening of a bitter wind. News came by a
myriad sources, carried secretly, passed from mouth to mouth.
Finally word of the Prince's whereabouts reached the fugitives.
He was on the coast at Arisaig.

Further intelligence proved vague and disquieting. Charles
designed to leave the country, had, in fact, been advised to do
so. Mr. Murray frowned. He proposed sending to the Prince
for orders and Dr. Cameron undertook the mission. On his
return his face and report were equally gloomy. Mr. Hay had
handled the interview. (Mr. Murray snorted.) He had refused
Dr. Cameron access to the Prince, but promised to try and
deliver any message with which Dr. Cameron was charged.
Hay was coldly informed that Dr. Cameron had instructions
to communicate his message to none save the Prince himself,
and thought it strange that his Royal Highness's whereabouts
should be kept a secret. He likewise hinted sharply that
Charles's intention of leaving Scotland was strongly disapproved of by his adherents.

Hay had wavered and hesitated. Dr. Cameron insisted on
knowing where the Prince was. Finally Hay offered to send a
messenger to find out what had become of Charles, but the
latter returned with such remarkable speed that Dr. Cameron
felt privately convinced that he had never gone as far as the
coast. His suspicions were further heightened by Mr. Hay's
going some distance to meet the man on his reappearance and
holding a long, private conversation with him. Ha! instruct-
ing him what to say, reflected the excellent doctor. The messenger's report, when suffered to give it, was that the Prince
had sailed from the mainland some hours previously.

Mr. Murray's remaining strength was dissipated in futile

wrath when Dr. Cameron related this intelligence. At first he refused to credit the news. Was it possible that any person about his Royal Highness could advise him to take so rash a step? he demanded incredulously. Hopeful that Charles was still on the mainland he composed a threatening letter to Mr. Hay, insisting that the bearer of it should be given immediate access to the Prince, but before the latter was half-way on his journey he encountered Hay, bound for Loch Arkaig.

A stormy interview ensued. Hay declared positively that the Prince was gone, and Sir Thomas Sheridan, appearing that night, corroborated the information. It was the more regretted as accounts came of two French ships being arrived with money, arms, and ammunition. Hay's impassioned insistence that he was innocent of having advised Charles to abandon the mainland and seek a doubtful safety in the islands, and that the Prince had indeed sailed before Dr. Cameron's arrival, was received by his predecessor with an ill grace and transparent disbelief, shared by the rest. What of the money? was universally asked.

Lochiel drew Murray of Broughton aside into one of the miserable huts which sheltered the fugitives.

"Sir, I am vastly unwilling to desert my clan in the unhappy situation we are now in. To do so would be inconsistent with my honour and their interest. You and I"—he smiled sadly —"have been hand-in-hand together during this whole affair. May I hope that you will not leave me, but we may share the same fate together?"

Murray consented. The gold was a fair lure. With the Prince gone and no one to claim it legally it ought to be used for those whom Charles's rashness had ruined. He proposed to the rest that every endeavour should be made to raise a body of men to continue the struggle, and Dr. Cameron and a relative, Major Kennedy, went off the same night to inform the officers to whom the gold had been entrusted that Murray was on his way to receive it. Scarcely able to stand upon his legs, as he ruefully described his condition, he started, but collapsing at Glendessary was obliged to spend a night there. The following day but one he arrived at Keppoch, opposite the bay where the ships lay at anchor.

The *Bellona* and the *Mars* had brought forty thousand *iouis d'ors*, the gold being packed in five large barrels, each nearly a yard long, in addition to arms and ammunition of all kinds. A number of fugitives from Culloden, and a large number of country people, had assembled at the spot. On a still May morning these watched with apprehensive eyes three English frigates, the *Greyhound*, the *Baltimore*, and the *Terror*, appearing in the bay. A long action was fought with the French vessels, ending in the latter's victory. They sailed again that evening with many of the fugitives on board, including the Duke of Perth, practically dying. The gold was landed and buried in a wood near Loch Arkaig.

It was May, but the weather continued wet, inclement, fitful. The little man, clad incongruously in the dress of a drover, shivered as he recalled recent nights. One had been spent in a goat-house, lying on the ground with a wheel-barrow for pillow; another in a sheiling. He was too unwell to walk. Horses—indifferent, rough-coated beasts—were with difficulty procured at incredible sums. Mr. Murray of Broughton learned what it was like to be a hunted man, a fugitive, one who could count upon no certain shelter or assistance. There was the minister who seemed so intimate with Captain McNabb's father. Mr. Murray had sent the latter with an offer of a hundred guineas if the man of God would conceal him for a fortnight. The answer, a brief refusal, made him mutter curses between his chattering teeth. After two nights in a remote country house Mrs. McNabb received a message that this was to be searched and it would be impossible to save any of the Prince's party found therein. Wearily Mr. Murray took the road again.

The river was so swollen that he crossed it with difficulty on horesback. A journey of four miles brought him to a sheiling in Balwhidder. Here he lingered until late the next day, when he set out at night, clad in old garments, and accompanied by Captain McNabb and Glencairnaig. The rain fell heavily, relentlessly, drenching him to the skin. At Stuart of Glenbucket's he halted for a couple of hours and then crossed a loch in the neighbourhood of Crieff to take up his quarters in an old barn. The wind whined persistently through the leaking timbers and the unceasing rain falling reminded him of gun-fire. A nightmare of an all-night ride followed. During the day, in the shelter of a MacGregor's house, he pondered desperately over the different routes he might take to reach his own neighbourhood. Stirlingshire? Mr. Murray pursed up his lips. The Government troops were quartered in Stirling and dispersed over the countryside. It was market-day, with many people on the road. Certain of these might recognize him, or, mistaking him for his assumed character, put questions to him which the sham drover would find mighty difficult to answer. The county was Whig, suspicious, on the watch for rebels, and the only house in which he might seek safety was too difficult to reach.

Linhouse? His aunt was married to Muirhead, the laird. Blood ran thicker than water. On the other hand, he was uncertain of the way. Too many inquiries might attract undesirable attention. Nor did he know whether anybody would be in the house excepting Mrs. Muirhead and her servants. She was eighty-two years of age and extremely deaf. Mr. Murray's pallor increased as he pictured himself discovering his real identity to her in a series of shouts which could only mean the whole household sharing in the secret. Additionally there were troops at Calder, barely two miles from Linhouse. No; Aunt Mary must be left in peace.

The third alternative was Tweeddale. He should avoid Edinburgh, where he was lamentably well known. His intention was to reach Polmood, his sister's house, with as little delay as possible, but the Fates seemed determined to vex him. His guide departed; the road was uncertain in the pitch-dark; his horse was almost falling under him. In despair he was compelled to stop at Killbucho. Another aunt resided here, but her husband and sons were from home. Soaking, exhausted, he plied the knocker. It was too dark, with rain and cloud, to see much of his surroundings as he stood in the cobbled courtyard, but memory painted for him with vivid brush the tall, white-harled L-shaped house, its crow-stepped gables, the glen beyond the garden, the burn and gean-trees——

"Maircy! wha's yon?"

"Cousin Bethia?"

"Wha are ye?"

The daughter of the house found it difficult to recognize her trim, perjink cousin, John Murray of Broughton, in the drookit individual, wearing a heavy coat and a blue bonnet. She stood in the hall, the draught blowing in all directions the flame of the candle she carried, her pretty mouth ajar.

"Hush! I do not wish my presence known. Pray, miss, do not use any ceremony lest it may give suspicion to the servants. Is my aunt within?"

"Ay, but——"

A door far down the hall opened. A tall, severe-faced, elderly Scottish gentlewoman, clad in a silk gown and a lace cap, emerged. She spoke her daughter's name sharply.

K

"Bethia! Whit's ta'n ye, crackin' an' daffin' at the door? Wha's wantin' in?"

"Mem, it is Co——"

Mr. Murray's ferocious frown and anguished gesture stopped the word in mid-career.

"I canna hear ye. I speired at ye wha is there?"

The supposed drover strode boldly in. He took off his dripping bonnet, which sent a spray of muddy raindrops in all directions.

"Ye impident gomeril!"

"Ma'am, I beg——"

"John! It's no' ye?"

Mrs. Dickson, by Scots courtesy Lady Killbucho, gazed in horror at her nephew. Bethia chirped and twittered in the background.

"Aunt, I regret my intrusion. Can you give me shelter for a few hours?"

She nodded dumbly. The catastrophe of Culloden was known to all. Many a family in Scotland awaited with dread tidings of the death, capture, or fate of kinsman. John had been high in the Prince's councils, an outstanding figure throughout the campaign. Lady Killbucho held no great opinion of his wife Margaret, making a spectacle of herself at the Mercat Cross such as no modest married woman should have done, but John was different. If he were taken——

"The soldiers are at Brochton Place," she whispered.

"I know. I must seek my sister at Polmood."

A rising wind flung the rain against the windows. The fugitive shuddered.

"Come away tae the dining-room an' I'll tell them tae bring ye a glass o' wine."

"You forget my guise, ma'am. A dram of whisky in the kitchen would be more suitable to my supposed condition."

"Na. Na. Ye maun be sairved fittingly."

There was no countering her snobbish obstinacy. Shivering with combined cold and apprehension, Mr. Murray followed the erect figure of his relative. A fire leaped in the wide grate and preparations for a substantial meal had been set out on the heavy oak table. The fugitive hung over the welcome warmth, furtively rubbing his clammy hands, whilst Lady Killbucho tugged at the bell-rope. A manservant answered the summons.

"Tammas! A glass o' claret immediately."

Mr. Murray stooped lower over the fire. The steam from his wet clothes filled the atmosphere with its reek.

"An' sairve denner. Ye'll tak' it beside us, John?"

The door shut upon the servant. Mr. Murray swung round, his face ashen.

"Ma'am, it is not wise. As you have ordered the wine, let me drink it and be gone."

"Tuts! There's nae danger."

"If you would permit me to eat and drink without service or ceremony——"

"Whit are ye feart o'?"

He did not answer. His thin shoulders drooped under the weight of the coarse, soaking cloak.

"There's a guid denner for ye. I'm blythe tae hae a man tae help Bethia an' me tae eat it. Yer Uncle William an' baith Bethia's brithers bein' away frae hame twa women canna manage a hen an' brose an' a gigot o' mutton an' a muckle great saumon, nae less. Sit ye doon an' use yer freedom."

"If I eat with you, ma'am, at least let me be called by another name. I might thus pass for a companion of your sons."

"Oh, ay. Mr. Tamson will dae fine. Bethia, ye'll mind tae ca' your cousin that?"

"Te be sure, mem. Mr. Tamson."

Bethia was giggling. She looked upon it as a jest, a ploy. His aunt nodded. To them it was nothing, a passing incident, but to himself——

The meal was heavy, ample, satisfying. Mr. Murray's thoughts strayed continually to his Prince. Where was Charles? What corner of the isles sheltered that hunted head? Thirty thousand pounds were set upon it. Many itching fingers would be stretched forth to grasp the sum——

"Cousin John, ye're no' eatin'?"

Bethia's shrill reminder interrupted his reverie. He glared at her and Lady Killbucho broke into a long account of her husband's recent losses at sheep-breeding.

"Indeed, ma'am? These are difficult times for such experiments."

"Ay. I tell't him it was a daft-like scheme—— Mr. Tamson, yer glass is toom. Whaur are yer wits, ye limmer?"

The last query was directed to the servant-lass who was waiting on the company. Mr. Murray's flesh grew cold as she leaned over and replenished his wine-glass. She was a sharp-featured, keen-eyed girl, and whilst she stood douce and attentive at the end of the room he had an uncomfortable idea that she strongly suspected a rebel was being entertained by her mistress. A queer-like drover, this, drinking claret and eating with the family as an equal——

He plunged desperately into talk.

"I regret heartily your younger son's absence, ma'am," he began.

"Oh, ay. Gin he had had word o' yer comin' nae doot he'd hae bided hame."

"Sure, you are no' verra gallant, Cousin—— La! I mean Mr. Tamson." Bethia was ogling him between the candles. "En't my mither an' me guid eneuch company?"

"Of course, miss. I merely meant that if your brother had been at home I would have persuaded him to take a jaunt to London that I might have the benefit of passing as his servant."

Bethia gaped at him.

"Oh, Cousin John! Whit a droll idea!"

"Haud yer fule's tongue!" snapped Lady Killbucho. "An' dinna wait, Isobel," she told the servant.

The door shut upon the girl. Mr. Murray shivered anew.

"I dinna understand," his aunt informed him.

"Well, ma'am, I am positive that that servant of yours suspects that I may be a rebel. I said that in order that if I find it convenient to stay any time in this country this pretended discovery of my scheme will be a means to make them believe that I have put it in execution, and thereby prevent any search for me in these parts."

"Och, Cousin John——"

"Will ye mind tae ca' him Mr. Tamson, ye daft lassie!"

"But he said Isobel suspected—— It's nae use ava pretendin' he's onybody but Murray o' Brochton."

"That was a sair-like defeat yer Prince had." Lady Killbucho helped herself to another slice of fowl, ignoring Bethia's protest. "When I heard o' it I thocht that nae mair could be done, but my nephew, Mr. William Lockhart, insisted that a' would gang well, and even sae lately as the preceding week he continued in the same way o' thinkin'."

"Indeed, ma'am?" Mr. Murray smiled sourly. "I wish it had been so, but Mr. Lockhart is vastly mistaken. I would not give a half-penny for any possibility that remained at present."

He stared gloomily before him. What prospect was there that the Prince would redeem his fortunes? The meeting of the chiefs at Muirlaggan on Loch Arkaig had led to nothing. Lord Lovat had boasted and promised. None of the clansmen who were to gather had ever done so. The leaders were scattered, Charles's followers in many instances prisoners or fugitives, the belated aid from France of no avail now. Mr. Murray's own plight was grievous. He would have preferred to spend the night at Killbucho and thus rest his horse as well as himself, but with soldiers at Broughton, only a mile distant, and the suspicions he felt had been awakened in the servant-lass's mind, it seemed wiser to shift his camp.

"I fear I should not linger, ma'am. I design to go to my sister Hunter at Polmood."

"It's owre late. They will a' be bedded."

"Perhaps my cousin would write a letter for me, ma'am, to acquaint my sister that I am coming."

Bethia was instantly all giggling acquiescence. She sat at the escritoire, her curls in danger of coming in contact with the candles, her small red tongue peeping out between her lips, her pen travelling over the paper. The letter was a harmless document, and even after it had been entrusted to a shock-headed lad about the place it carried no danger.

Between nine and ten Mr. Murray set out. The rain had slackened and was almost ceasing. A wind blew coldly over the fields and sighed amongst the trees. He rode steadily, encouraging his jaded beast, himself almost as weary. The faces of his aunt and cousin danced before his eyes. Every bush held an enemy. His body, sodden with fatigue, enfeebled by illness, craved only for the repose of a clean bed, and the refreshment of sound, dreamless sleep. The miles stretched endlessly. It was two hours before he saw the lights of Polmood and fell from his saddle at the door. A woman was waiting——

"John! Brother!"

"I am spent. Let me lie down."

"But your safety—— Does any know that you are here?"

He shook his head stupidly.

Mrs. Hunter brought him upstairs. She had sent her servants to bed, and whispered that he was safe. Together they concerted that the following day she should dispatch an express to Edinburgh for his brother-in-law, who would engage a ship to take Mr. Murray over to France. Until then he must rest and recover his depleted strength——

At Broughton a servant-lass asked to see the captain in command of the soldiers quartered there. He came, yawning and loudly incredulous, to hear her tale. Mr. Murray had supped at Killbucho and set out for Polmood betwixt nine and ten? Was she daft or dreaming? Isobel M'Kerral repeated her story with such detail and conviction that he began to think there might be something in it. A man wearing a jocky coat and a blue bonnet was scarce likely to be given a glass of wine and entertained to dinner unless he were other than he seemed. And miss had called him "Cousin John"? Ha! ha!

At two in the morning a sudden noise awakened Mr. Murray from his slumbers. The dragoons were at the gate.

CHAPTER XXIV

THE WIND WHICH HAD CRIED ALL DAY WAS DROPPING TO A THIN whine, like a fretful bairn who has tired his puny strength too greatly for more tears. The air was full of autumn scents and sounds: the rustle of fallen leaves, the haste of rain-swollen water, the acrid tang of burned branches. Dusk was draping the landscape, a foreign panorama, alien in aspect and association to the man who walked wearily through the sodden woods. He hoarded a few coins, sufficient to pay for a night's lodging, and carried his worldly possessions in a bundle on his back.

The one lamp-lit window of the inn showed like a bright eye out of the blackness that framed it. The traveller stumbled forward, his heart and step lighter for the prospect of shelter and food. Seen nearer, the place was like hundreds of other foreign inns in the eighteenth century. It sat low to the ground, and the rotting window-frames and mean door in the centre cried out for paint. The newcomer, impatient, hammered on the peeling wood with a rough stick.

The man who came to answer the imperious summons bore a fugitive likeness to the intending guest. Each was tall, big-boned, with a lean, hollow-eyed face and long, spare limbs. The Continent had given grudged shelter and sanctuary to both, but they had been cradled and bred up in a land of mist and heather, of high mountains and deep, black-bosomed lochs, a land of fierce loves and fiercer hates, of undying loyalty to a dwindling dynasty, and secret, bitter rebellion against the unyielding yoke of a usurper. The two dour faces confronting one another lightened the least fraction.

"A wild night." The traveller spoke in the Gaelic. "Have you shelter—food and a bed? I can pay."

"All three." The landlord drew back a pace. "Ay, but it would be wilder on the road between Ben Druh and Skellig-mohr."

The guest sighed. "So you know that bit of Scotland?"

"Ask a man if he knows the face which looks at him daily from his mirror."

"My mirror was aye the burn that runs through the fields below my father's croft."

"Ay, and in winter storms, when the melted snow had swollen it, it spoke night-long."

"There are streams and torrents in this country, but their speech is strange and unfriendly."

The landlord led the way into an empty room. A wood fire glowed, showing the mean appointments of the place, the squalor, dust, and disorder. The wind had risen again suddenly. It beat and howled against the windows. From overhead there came the sound of loud snoring.

"You have another guest?"

"He need not trouble you. He said that a bottle of wine was all the supper he should require." The innkeeper moved about, setting a rough meal upon the table. "You would see Scotland again?" he asked abruptly.

The other shrugged his shoulders. "Inquire of any Christian if he would see Heaven." He paused. "For me, there is no going back."

"Seven years soften memories."

"Ay—and deepen the edge of hate. Does the Government sleep?"

The landlord was bending over the fire. "If the Government is your only foe——"

The exile, huddled in a chair, failed to notice the suspicion sharpening the watching face.

"What should take me back, hunted and landless?" he demanded wearily. "Seven years ago I saved my neck at the price of banishment and poverty. My chief lies dead—dead of heart-break, though they cried it the foul air of Paris and the canker of unhealed wounds from Culloden. Why should I go back?"

"Your chief?"

"Donald Cameron of Lochiel, the fair-haired one."

"There are still Camerons."

"For me only Lochiel's son, and he is but a child."

"Lochiel's brother lives."

The Cameron laughed bitterly.

"Fassefern the cautious? Did he not beg our chief to hold back when Prince Charles landed? Well, he knew that the

Rising would smoulder out like burning leaves under rain if Lochiel refused to join."

"There is another than Fassefern."

"Archibald? The doctor who had better have left politics alone and kept to his trade of leech and healer?"

The man who owned the inn inquired sharply: "Why should you say that?"

The guest's smile was bleak. "It was Archibald Cameron who helped to bury the bags of gold on which the curse lies heavy."

The landlord muttered: "Ay—but the bags are lighter."

The warmth of the room began to creep over the numbed limbs of the Cameron. He sat more erect and his eyes grew angry. "May the curse fall on those who dipped their fingers in that gold!" he cried fiercely.

"What of the man who helped Dr. Cameron to lay it in the earth?"

"Murray of Broughton? Ay, he had the fingering of it, but it brought him little good. Men spit at his name, and even the old fox at Castle Downie they said showed more of a man at his trial than the wretch Murray who testified against him."

"Where is he now?"

"None knows. He took the Government's pay and slunk from the haunts of honest men."

"But the gold?"

"It was for the Prince and for the Cause."

"The Cause is dead, and the Prince no man knows where."

"Did you ever see him?"

The landlord shook his head.

"I did. Never shall I forget that face and that smile. I was one of the seven hundred clansmen Lochiel gathered to march behind him to Glenfinnan. The Prince was standing amongst the men who sailed with him, Irish, Catholic, landless, save for the old one who was chief of the Atholl Murrays."

"You mean Lord George, whom the Prince aye hated?"

"No. His shadow fell later. This was Tullibardine, the exiled for thirty years. They say that he wept when he saw the black coast of Scotland again."

The landlord scowled. "Take your supper and forget these old sorrows."

"Only when the earth of this hostile country covers me, and perhaps not then, can I forget. I had thought to lie under heather, but——" He broke off. "Was that someone stirring overhead?"

"My other guest. He has his bottle and as soft a bed as I could provide. He will not disturb us."

"A traveller?"

"Ay. A Scotsman, by his look, though he has no Gaelic. You spoke of the Prince?"

"He stole my heart with one smile. It did not matter that we could not follow his speech, and he knew naught but a few stumbling syllables of ours. We loved him and served him—to the end."

"Culloden?"

"Ay. That dark morning. It broke the heart of Scotland. I was more fortunate than many in that I gained France, but seven years are long."

"You have sought no pardon?"

"Never!"

The silence gathered again, only broken by that vehement wind outside——

"You, too, served and lost, I take it?" the Cameron asked.

"Should I be here otherwise?"

"I do not know. There is a tale of a man who stood by when the French gold was carried up the beach. He kept a still tongue, but his eyes were everywhere. One bag was missing, after they counted the whole. *Who was that man?*"

"How should I tell? Ask your chief's brother—and the rest who meddled in the thing."

The Cameron went on monotonously:

"The gold was tied in bags and buried in a wood. At dead of night four came from Lochiel's house of Achnacarry and bore the burden of it under a moon which saw all but could prove nothing. There were human eyes which watched as well. Ewan MacPherson, whose clan calls him thief and traitor, lightened that hidden gold by many a *louis d'or*."

"Your supper will be cold, Cameron."

"Let it lie there! Would I defile my lips by touching food that your treacherous hands have prepared? Seven years! Ay, but my exile was honourable. What of yours?"

The innkeeper, cringing, asked fearfully: "How did you know me?"

"Has your coward's face changed so greatly? I heard the tale in Paris, whispered by other exiles' lips. You, who hung back when the Prince needed every claymore, who put his croft before the Cause, is it not enough that you failed your King's son, but you must rob him in addition?"

The man thus addressed and accused mumbled defiance.

"It was afterwards. The Prince had gone from Scotland, and there were many who prayed that he might not come again. The gold lay rusting under the earth, there for the taking of any who knew the secret of where it lurked. If it had not been I, there were others whose fingers itched for it, ay, and lifted it——"

"Why did you not bide in Scotland? Did shame force you to seek a foreign land—or fear?"

"Both. There were whispers, and I had no liking for a dirk between my shoulder-blades. I bought this inn, but it has never prospered."

"Did you deserve that it should?"

Across the room there came the slow defence.

"One man ruined a nation. Was it so great a crime to take a handful of his gold by way of repayment, recompense?"

"To whom? To you, who neither sacrificed nor suffered aught for Tearlach?"

The landlord said stumblingly: "If I have stolen, I have paid. Think you, Neil Cameron, that it is a little thing to slink about with bowed head, fearful of any from Scotland who might—know? Do you believe that I have never lain wakeful o' nights, sick for the peat-reek and the wind over bog-myrtle and rushes? I saw in your eyes that you knew me and knew my shame, but for the sake of speaking for an hour in my own tongue I risked your knowledge. What shall ye do with me?"

The Cameron spoke dully. "I vowed, if ever Fate should set us face to face, that it would be your life or mine. Now you have tied my hands. That stolen gold has brought your punishment. If I should see the Prince again my eyes could meet his, unafraid. What of you?"

The loud banging of a door overhead startled both. A thick, drunken voice was raised in song. Stumbling footsteps came down the wooden stair. The two men sat watchful. The sounds rang nearer, and presently the strayed reveller lurched into the room.

He was a man who looked some forty years of age, but might very possibly be less. Excesses of all kinds had stolen his youth. His complexion was blotched and patchy; his eyes, originally a brilliant brown, were glazed and suspicious. Once slim, tall, erect, he had grown stooped, paunchy, and heavy of tread. He slumped down slackly into a chair and leered at the two Scots.

"Your wine is thin stuff, landlord." His voice was querulous. "Have you nothing stronger to warm a traveller on a night like this?"

"There is brandy, monsieur."

"Bring it here!" The order was imperious.

The innkeeper set fresh glasses and a squat-necked bottle on the table.

With a shaking hand the stranger poured out the amber contents. "You will pledge me?" he asked the Cameron.

The latter stood up silently. "I have but one toast." He held his glass high. "To the Prince who hid in the heather, and for whom Scotland still waits!" he cried.

The half-drunken man set down his brandy untasted. "Another!" he muttered. Then aloud: "You followed—and lost all?"

"I was but one of many. And you?"

"I staked and lost all." He shrugged his shoulders. "Our host does not drink. You have no sympathy with a fallen Cause and an exiled Prince, perhaps?"

The answer came scornfully. "I have no use for a land under a usurper's heel, and a Stuart who seeks to forget in brandy what he cost Scotland."

The man addressed stared vaguely. "Is that how Scotland speaks of—Tearlach?"

The room was suddenly quiet save for the drip of liquid from an overturned glass.

"No!" Neil Cameron cried the word, the defiance. "Scotland has never forgotten how she gave her heart. The Prince came, trusting Scotland, and in the long months of hiding, hunted, he learned what that trust was worth. Was there a man who would have taken the Government's price, gold set upon a golden head?"

The wanderer's hand sought vaguely for the half-empty bottle. "A nation of fools!" he shouted. "Wealth for a clan, a fortune for an individual, yet none of you would put out his finger——" He broke off. "And with such men, such loyalty, he failed—failed!"

Neil Cameron said swiftly: "Is it failure to have won—and kept—the love and faith of Scotland? Were he to come again, we would follow him to a man!"

The stranger spoke thickly. "You loved and served him seven years back. Would you say the same if you could see him as he is to-day? The Prince who swayed Scotland with a smile—what is he now? A drunkard, a sot, the toy of light women, who tempts Fate time and again by mad plots which dissolve into rainbow bubbles, leaving nothing but soured hopes. Would Scotland serve such an one?"

The eyes of Neil Cameron were bright with anger. "Who are you, to dare to defame the Prince?" he demanded. "Were you with him through his campaign?"

The other laughed bitterly. "Ay. I was with him from the hour he trod Scottish soil until the night he stole from it, a defeated failure. I know of what I speak. If you saw him now, you would not recognize him, and when you did, you would shrink from him."

"Never! I should know him amid thousands, and follow him again to the world's end!"

The drink-sodden wreck swayed to his feet. He laughed terribly and flung a handful of coins on the table. "Take your reckoning, landlord," he gasped. "I cannot stay. The wild night is kinder." He stumbled towards the door. "Do not heed for me. I have been abroad in worse weather, a price upon my head, soaking heather for my couch, but good friends, as hard-pressed as myself, for company. Would to God Cumberland's red-coats had taken me then!"

The door slammed after him and the clamour of wind and rain drowned his departing footsteps. Neil Cameron sat still, dazed. "Who was he?" he stammered. "Once or twice—— The smile—— That lift of the head—— It cannot be. Tearlach!"

The innkeeper's mouth lengthened in a sneering grin. "And for—that, Scotland sits ruined," he mocked. "That—wreck!"

The next second he found himself rolling on the floor, the Cameron's hands clutching his throat.

"You do well to scoff, you, who first robbed him, and then let him go from your house!" he cried passionately. "Where were my eyes that I did not know him, even after seven years? My Prince, my Prince, come back!"

He snatched open the door and listened long, but nothing answered him except the wind's wailing.

THE END

"O Clans of the Gaels
   Who ever were loyal,
   Horo, make ready to go;
And give service now
   Faithful to Charles,
   Horo, make ready to go.
Serve him each one
   Without any delay,
Read not your danger
   But in Christ put your trust;
Proudly and noisily,
Well-equipped, stormily,
Eager to go with him,
Ardent and valorous,
   Horo, make ready to go.

Ere you take your departure
   Bid farewell to your comrades,
   Horo, make ready to go;
Bid farewell to your wives,
   Your houses, your treasure,
   Horo, make ready to go.
Let each man be twain
   When the time comes for fighting,
Each arm well-sinewed,
   Each heart as a lion's;
Fiercely and wildly,
Ready-handed and boldly,
On each field be triumphant,
Wherever you chance to be,
   Horo, make ready to go."

Angus MacDonald, *c.* 1665-1745, translated by John Lorne
   Campbell from *Oran Brosnachaidh do na Gaidheil* in *Highland Songs of the Forty-five.*